GW00717050

Just (Enough) Grace (For a Vicar's Wife)

Grace Hulbert

New Millennium
292 Kennington Road, London SE11 4LD

British Library Cataloguing in Publication Data.
A catalogue record for this book is obtainable
from the British Library.

Printed and bound by Watkiss Studios Ltd.
Biggleswade, Beds.
Issued by New Millennium*
ISBN 1 85845 265 1
*An imprint of The Professional Authors' & Publishers' Association

This book is affectionately dedicated to
Monica Priestman
whose love and support meant so much to Grace in her latter
years and whose generosity has made publication possible

Grace Hulbert (1947)

iv

CONTENTS

FOREWORD

I was privileged to know Grace Hulbert for only the last few years of her life, but this was quite long enough for me to perceive and appreciate two major qualities in her – enthusiasm and faith.

Grace's enthusiasm was infectious. She never ceased to be deeply interested and absorbed in the events and people that she encountered and this habit of fascination seemed to add extra light and optimism to the very atmosphere of situations that she became part of. Without doubt also, as you will discover while reading this book, she stored away these memories and impressions of people and places, the fruits of her abiding fascination, in such a way that they could be easily retrieved when she decided to offer this gift of the story of her life to so many people.

Grace's faith was the faith of a child, although not the faith of a foolish child. I have rarely met anyone with a more transparently genuine belief in the power and love of God, but, as you will see, her faith passed through more than one fire of testing, and emerged on each occasion in a deeper and more authentic form. I should be pleased to go to my maker with one tenth of the humble confidence which characterised Grace's trust in Jesus at the end of her life.

The burning desire to write came quite late in life, but when it did come it arrived on the wings of a passion that full-time writers will completely understand. Grace wanted to know everything there was to know about the business of planning a book, writing it, getting it published and how it would be distributed once it was ready for the marketplace. I seemed to recall that, even before she had written a single chapter, she was asking me how much I thought it should be priced at in the local Christian bookshop.

The book that Grace has written is full of love and smiles, with a trace of pain and heart-ache thrown in, because that is the way of the real world, whether one is a Christian or not, and Grace always lived in a real world. It is the story of a life that has been led rather in the manner of the old disciples, who were far from sure where they were going or why they were going there, but had the good sense to follow Jesus anyway. It is a good read and a good and inspiring testimony. I pray that you will enjoy it as much as I have.

Adrian Plass
May 1999

CHAPTER 1
EARLY DAYS

I have come very close to death. Perhaps that is why I am putting pen to paper now. In the past, friends had said, "You should write a book", but time and space were hard to find. Involved with my husband Hugh in the work of a parish, with so much going on around us, life was rich and full, but there were no spare days. Our three children added a depth to parish life that spread far beyond the family. At times I felt that the Church of England did very well from the Hulbert clan, five for the price of one!

I have always believed that people are more important than things, and as a vicar's wife have met with "all sorts and conditions" of people. As someone once said, 'God must love ordinary people very much, He made so many of them'. Or as Martin Luther put it, "God does not love us because we are valuable, but we are valuable because God loves us", and that includes me, a very ordinary person, but one who believes in an extraordinary God.

Having written down my experiences during the last few years I read them to our daughter Ruth. Her comment was: "Mum, you cannot start there, you have to start at the beginning." So that is what I'm doing, starting at the beginning, and calling my book "Just (enough) Grace" (for a vicar's wife). Because without God's grace, there would be no book and no author, and for so much of my life I have been 'the vicar's wife'. It is all here - the love and the fear, the joy and the pain, the peace and the worry, the praise and the thanksgiving - indeed the fullness of living Life with a capital "L" in Jesus.

I was born on July 7th, 1926, an early birthday present for my mother, whose birthday was on the 10th. To me, July is the best month of the year and I feel sorry for anyone whose birthday does not fall in that month. In spite of this my three children were born in March, February, and January respectively! My birth date is easy to remember, 7.7.26, but on my seventh

1

birthday there was a problem, I was born on the seventh day of the seventh month in 1926 and not 1927. As far as I was concerned I had been born in the wrong year! I can still remember telling mother it was her fault!

When the Aunt, who was to be one of my godmothers visited me, (so I'm told), I was asleep in the cot, a contented baby with a lot of dark hair. She picked me up and said, "What a little joy - you must call her Joy." My parents were not so sure about Joy and decided on Joyce, but before I had any say in things, they had settled on my second name, Grace, a family name, and Grace it has been ever since!

With my younger brother John, I had a happy childhood, but then the war came. Everything changed and we went to stay with an uncle and aunt in Bedfordshire. My mother and father survived the bombing in south-east London, but we have family and friends who did not. When I was at school and looked at a map of the world, a good proportion was pink, a comforting thought at such a time, if you were British. At last the war ended and everyone was happy, but amid the jubilation I noticed sad folk, those whose loved ones had not returned, and many who came back still bearing the scars of war and the suffering they had endured.

I began work as a Civil Servant up in the City and John was called up for national service in the army. Before the end of the war, I decided to go back to the church we had been to as children, and met many old friends. St John's, Deptford, is just above the station of that name, and a landmark on the Lewisham High Road, or Lewisham Way as it now is, the A 21 route into the City.

As young people, we had lots of energy, and a very wise Vicar, Canon Livermore, who got us all involved in the life of the church. I started attending the prayer and Bible study meeting, but never prayed aloud, thinking everyone else was much better at praying than I was, and my prayers were not really important. I became interested in missionary work again; this had been important to me, even as a child in Sunday School.

2

Under the leadership of Dorothy, who had been my teacher in earlier days, I began teaching in the Sunday School.

Our Vicar was a gifted pastor and excelled at finding work for his young people. One day he asked me if I would take an old lady out in her wheelchair, she needed to get fresh air and meet other people. She was quite heavy and pushing the wheelchair was hard going, with a hill to negotiate. We went down to Lewisham Market where there was much activity for her to enjoy, and before long we were both ready for tea and cakes. However the wheelchair made access impossible for the place I had in mind, so I pushed her along a path, lined with shops on one side and the market on the other, until we reached a street cafe with a few tables and a bar counter to order from. Not quite what I had in mind but I could push the chair up to a table, while I went to give my order. When I got back to the table I saw tears in the old lady's eyes, I was concerned, but she said she was all right. It puzzled me. Why the tears? Surely she had enjoyed the afternoon. What was wrong? I know now that we can shed tears of happiness and relief from tension, and we can shed tears just because somebody cares, and I had cared. That's all that is left of the memory - where I met the lady and what her name was I do not recall, but the lesson learned that day was much more than how to push an old lady in a wheelchair!

It was about this time that I made a personal commitment to follow Jesus. My joy was complete: I had peace with God through Jesus Christ, and this was a day by day experience. Hugh has just read this sentence and his comment is, "I would amplify that a bit." He is right, so here goes.

On the first Remembrance Sunday after the war had ended, I went with a friend who was still in the W.A.A.F., to a parade service at "Dear old St John's", as we have since come to call it. The church was packed, the Mayor and other dignitaries were seated in the front pew, and a special preacher had been invited. Colonel W.E. Shewell-Cooper was well known through his many books on horticultural subjects, but he was supremely

3

a man with a great desire to bring others to Christ. The service was full of praise and I was thrilled to be able to say thank you to God for keeping our family safe through the war. I have no idea what Shewell-Cooper said, but at the end of the sermon he made an appeal and said, "If you want to know Jesus as your personal Saviour, will you please come out to the front and receive a booklet from me." The Church was quiet and still, no one moved, I wondered why. Surely someone in this congregation wanted to say thank you to God for all His goodness and protection during the war? A voice inside me said "How about you?" I realised then that something more than saying thank you would be required of me if I went forward, I would be committing myself to a way of life in Jesus Christ. Still no one moved. I was shy and did not want to get on my feet with so many people around and my friend alongside. Suddenly it was all so clear, I knew I loved Jesus, this had been coming on for weeks, and the simple question, "Do you want to know Jesus as your personal Saviour?" had brought it to a head. I knew I loved Jesus and wanted to say so publicly, and I was on was on my feet and walking forward before I realised it. No one else moved. My footsteps seemed so loud. I saw Canon Livermore looking at me with a wonderful smile on his face, and then to my amazement he gave me a wink! I heard other feet making their way up the aisle; altogether thirteen of us gave our lives to the Lord Jesus Christ that morning.

The Vicar arranged a house party at Fairlight Hall in East Sussex, and there I met Hugh Hulbert, who was just starting a degree course at Bristol University in preparation for the ordained ministry. The house party was a great success. We had a week of fun, laughter, good food, walks and enjoyment in each other's company. During the war our beaches were mined and out of bounds, with barbed wire everywhere, but now we were able to roam around just as we pleased, walk on the sands, paddle or swim, the war was over and we were free. I was just twenty, at peace with the world, and very happy in my new found Christian faith.

We still had coupons for food and clothes, but one could eat out and nylons were just beginning to filter through. My brother John sent me some from Germany where he was based on an American airfield. They were the first seamless ones I had come across and could be mended for about one shilling, or five pence. During the holiday Hugh would tease me and pull my leg (without the nylons of course as it was summer) but as I was aware, he was a student preparing for ordination and so I treated him with great respect. When we left Fairlight he offered to carry my case and (without my knowledge) copied my address from the label and started writing to me. We had so much in common and the friendship grew, but in no way did I want to become a vicar's wife. Bear in mind that I am writing of fifty years ago. Vicar's wives took meetings, prayed extemporarily, chaired committees, had their hair in buns and wore lisle stockings. I had short hair, wore nylons and enjoyed the "New Look." I had never taken a meeting in my life! We talked and prayed this over, Hugh said he loved me as I was, and so, for better or worse, he asked my father if he could marry his daughter and Dad said Yes.

My parents loved their future son-in-law, and even before our marriage he became one of the family. I also grew to love my future in-laws and their family in Bognor. Hugh had two brothers, two sisters and lots of maiden aunts. Earlier his family had worshipped at Holy Trinity, Eastbourne, where Canon S.M. Warner prepared him for confirmation.

Just before the war he had started training to be a quantity surveyor in Eastbourne. In 1940 he moved to London, where, at his father's suggestion, he made contact with St John's Deptford, and was greatly encouraged to find that Canon Warner was conducting a Tent Mission there at the time! Later he went to Moreton-in-Marsh (made famous by "Much Binding" on the radio), to work on an airfield. He recalls that his landlady never gave him a second course for Sunday dinner and he missed his mother's home cooking. He mentioned this to his landlady and next Sunday had roast beef, two veg., Yorkshire pudding and gravy followed by Yorkshire pudding and jam! The war brought many changes, but most people took them in their stride.

In 1942 he was called up into the army. The then vicar of St John's, Guthrie Clark, gave all young men going into the forces a stamped addressed postcard, to be returned once they had witnessed for Christ in the barrack room, by openly reading their Bible and praying. I think that took courage! Yes - he received his postcard from Hugh after a few days.

A year later, there was another call, to serve God in the ordained ministry. At the end of the war, Hugh was given an early release and changed battle dress for student's gown. It was at this point that I came into his life, and the Post Office delivered many letters to the Bible Churchmen's College, Bristol, on my behalf. I remember Dad Hulbert telling me he had prayed that one of his sons would go into the ministry. "The fervent prayer of a righteous man availeth much." So many things constituted Hugh's call, among them are prayer, Bible reading, encouragement from friends and family, but above all, the willingness to say yes to the Lord.

We became engaged on the 13th September 1947, and wanted to marry at the end of Hugh's degree course two years later. We decided to put the engagement ring on in St Paul's Cathedral. During my lunch hour, in college vacations, we had often sat on the steps of St Paul's listening to the band. I wonder if this is still part of City life or have cutbacks brought their gloomy change? Would people stop to listen now anyway? Civil Servants worked on Saturday morning in those days. When we arrived at St.Paul's we were met with such crowds, it was impossible to find a quiet place, so we decided to climb the stairs, eventually coming to the whispering gallery. Hardly the place to become engaged, and the gallery was crowded, so we made our way to the balcony outside, knowing that not many people ventured that far.

We looked out over a London, still showing the scars of bombing, not a pretty sight. Hugh asked, "Are you willing to go anywhere with me, wherever God leads us?" My answer was yes. We both knew God had brought us together, and that we could trust Him for the future, whatever it might hold.

The big moment had come, but just as Hugh started to put the ring on, the clock began to strike the hour, and as it boomed away we could only look at each other and laugh, and wait until St Paul's had finished striking and given us its blessing! Our second son is called Paul. (Have I ever told you this story, Dear?) It seems that many precious memories are brought to the surface, once one starts writing a book.

So there we were, young and eager to get married, neither of us approving of long engagements. Hugh sent a letter to the Church authorities, telling them what we proposed. The reply came back saying in effect that if we went ahead with our plans to marry before the ordination course was completed Hugh's Church grant would be withdrawn. This was a blow, but as Hugh needed the grant, we had to accept the decision. The letter was from the Church's Advisory Council for Training for the Ministry, CACTM for short, and it was signed, "John Phillips, Secretary."

"If ever I meet John Phillips I will tell him just what I think of him," I said.

Did I ever forgive John Phillips? Yes I did. It seems a good idea to skip a few years and tell you how.

Hugh became vicar of St Luke's, Southsea, in 1963. The Church had been through more than a year's interregnum, not surprising, because it was in a down town area with many small houses, due for demolition, and everything was at a low ebb. We had only been in the vicarage a few weeks, when I had a letter from Mrs Phillips, the Bishop's wife, asking me to make sure her husband had a midday rest when he came to visit our parish in a few weeks time. This was the first we had heard of the Bishop's proposed visit, and everyone was quite excited.

John Phillips had not been in Portsmouth very long and planned to visit every church in the diocese, an excellent idea, but very tiring, especially as the clergy (and their wives) tried to show him everything in one day. He arrived home exhausted. I wrote and assured Mrs Phillips we had planned a midday rest for her husband.

The great day came and after lunch we sat chatting. John Phillips was a warm-hearted man, obviously interested in his clergy and their families. He asked me if we had met, prior to the induction.

"No," I said, "we have not met before, but we once had a letter from you that caused us great distress."

He sat straight up in his chair, leaned forward and asked me about it. When I had explained he said that he was sorry, but as secretary to CACTM he had to sign letters, whether he agreed with the contents or not. I told him all was forgiven, and accepted his apology! When it was time for his rest I said he could put his feet up on our sofa. At first, he said no, but later, as I passed the window, I saw his feet sticking out over the end of our long settee.

I had kept my promise to Mrs Phillips, but I had also said my piece!

We were married on the 15th July 1950, at the end of Hugh's training, St Swithin's day, and it rained! The new Vicar of St John's, Bill Lee, took our marriage service. The opening hymn, 'Love Divine', to the tune 'Blaenwern', which was just getting popular, nearly raised the roof and set the tone for a wonderful service. How could it have been otherwise with that great lady, Mrs Keylock, at the organ!

Fifteen years later in Portsmouth we met up with Mrs Keylock again. She was still the same and to my mind had hardly changed. She still carried her flat shopping bag and always had something in it for the children, usually chocolate. I have a memory of her sitting at our kitchen table, with our three children, Martin, Paul and Ruth, hovering around, wondering what she had got for them this time.

We took her into the church, as she was keen to see the organ. Hugh asked her, "Would you like to play?" She answered, "Yes please, I would, but you go and sit in the pews and I'll play for you." We sat down, and, to our amazement, she started playing the tunes she had played at our wedding, ending with a fine rendering of the Wedding March. It was wonderful to hear her play again, she knew she had given us great pleasure. I asked her "How did you remember our wedding hymns?" She said, "I have remembered most of the tunes our young people chose for their weddings."

As children she had trained us to sing for the Sunday School Anniversary. I can remember her now, sitting down at the piano, with, of course, her flat bag somewhere around. Now I am looking forward to hearing her making wonderful music with her harp! A wonderful child of God who gave back to Him, in full, the gift He had given her.

Bill spoke on a text we had chosen, "Heirs together of the grace of life", from 1 Peter 3 v. 7. A friend sang while we signed the registers and soon we were sailing down the aisle to the triumphant notes of the Wedding March.

I must tell you here of a little incident which took place a month or so later. Hugh and I went up to a rally at the Central Hall, Westminster, and arrived a few minutes late to the sound of hearty singing to that same tune 'Blaenwern'. "We had this at our wedding," said my husband proudly to the young man giving out the hymn books, and we hurried in to take our places. Turning the pages over we found ourselves singing,

"Souls of men why will you scatter,
Like a crowd of frightened sheep?"

Funny hymn for a wedding, the young man must have thought!

Our reception, with a hundred or so friends and relatives, was held in the church hall, just along the road. Just before we were due to leave I missed one of my bridesmaids, Hugh's younger sister, Angela. I found her in the cloakroom, crying as if her heart would break. What - tears on my wedding day, "What is wrong dear, please tell me?" I asked. She looked at me, and said, smiling through her tears, "Oh Grace, I'm so happy!"

We got what was known as the "Honeymoon special" from Waterloo, couples and confetti in almost every compartment, and arrived at Wroxall on the Isle of Wight three hours later. At the Christian Guest House there, we were greeted at the gate by some young people with yet more confetti. How did they know? It's quite a story. Hugh had written to book us in and the envelope, with his college crest on the back, had been reused by the proprietor to answer another enquiry, for the same week as ours, from the parents of a fellow student at Bristol. When he saw the envelope, he put two and two together and our secret was out! Perhaps it was just as well that Percy did not accompany his parents on holiday that year!

My mother and I had talked about Hugh's need of a desk, as I planned to buy him one for an Ordination present. Those I had seen in the shops were expensive and not, to my mind, very suitable. In clergy studies I had seen were good-sized desks with plenty of drawers and a big flat top. We let things ride until one morning, when, right out of the blue, mother said, "Let's go down to Douglas Street, we might find a desk."

It meant quite a long walk into Deptford to a Saturday market. Food stalls were piled high with fruit and vegetables, groceries and meat, and there were white elephant stalls with all sorts of odds and ends, some new, some second hand. Larger items were set out in the road. Bargains galore, if you were prepared to bargain! We walked down the busy, noisy street, everyone selling their wares, - and there it was in the road, just the desk I was looking for. "How much?" I asked the stall-holder. "Five pounds" he said. "No, too much," I replied and walked away, saying to mother, "He will never sell that desk here." Some half an hour later we came back. "Not sold the desk yet?" I said; the man could only answer no. I went over and had another look. The drawers had LCC - for London County Council - stamped on the locks. A good sign, I thought, it looked solid and durable. "I'll buy it for three pounds ten shillings - if you will deliver it," I said. Another "No." "Take it or leave it," I replied, "You'll never sell that desk down here." I walked away again. Mother thought I was pushing too hard, perhaps she was right! But his voice followed me clearly, "OK.

10

Miss, it's a deal. You've got a bargain there." Yes I had. The desk was delivered to my parent's home and Dad did a fine repair and polishing job on it. In the family it is still affectionately known as 'Douglas'. We could not part with it, even in retirement and moving to a bungalow. The best three pounds fifty pence I ever spent!

Hugh was ordained on the 1st October 1950, in Southwark Cathedral. We were allowed two tickets for the service. My mother-in-law and I were early, but even so, were allocated seats in a side aisle at the back. We could not see much of the activities up at the front, but could hear quite well. While saying the Creed, when we came to, "He suffered and was buried", everyone around us knelt; this made quite a noise, as most people leaned on their chairs to get down. Mother and I were the only ones left standing in our area. I wondered what was going on; then, with more noise from the chairs, they all got to their feet again as they said, "On the third day He rose again from the dead." We did not do that at St John's!

When I heard the name 'Hugh Forfar Hulbert' called, I felt so proud of my husband. At this point in the service I dedicated myself afresh to God for whatever ministry He had for me as Hugh's wife. I was deeply moved by this experience. We have always been "Heirs together of the grace of God." Our marriage has always been a partnership, in every way.

Cutting the Cake on St. Swithun's Day 1950

The Family at Romford in 1959

CHAPTER 2
SOMEWHERE TO LIVE

Hugh's first curacy was at St.Mary's, Summerstown, in south-west London, not a well-known church, but we have lovely memories of our time spent there. Cecil Collins, a friend from college days, had entered the ministry later in life and needed a young curate. All he had to offer was work! No accommodation, not a good stipend (we started at £200 a year), but fellowship and friendship in the gospel was there in abundance. We liked Cecil and his wife Daisy and got on well together. They were a loving, caring couple, but did not have any children.

Our most urgent need was somewhere to live, but every avenue we tried fell through. We even went to the local council, with Cecil, to see if we could get a prefab. These were prefabricated bungalows, built after the war, to ease the housing shortage as men were released from the forces. Accommodation was at a premium, and we had little money, but although we were trusting God, nothing happened! A friend, a young war widow, said we could share her flat in Wimbledon, we took her up on her offer and stayed with Rhoda for about four months. She was wonderful, and we have much to thank her for, but obviously this was not a long-term solution. We were still on food coupons; I collected them every month from the Town Hall, as we did not have a permanent address. After four months I knew something had to be done. We talked and prayed things over and felt I should not get any more temporary food coupons. I would go home to my parents and get a job; Hugh could easily get accommodation in the parish - without me. It was a hard decision to face, but we both knew Hugh had been called to St Mary's.

Just before the food coupons ran out Hugh came home really excited. There was the possibility of two rooms in Vanderbilt Road, Earlsfield, in a neighbouring parish. Hugh went to see the landlady. She did not take the chain off the door as it was dark, but said that she would see us the following day. We told her later she was right not to take the chain off the door and she laughed and said she had no idea Hugh was a clergyman, she had not opened the door enough to see his clerical collar. Kathleen was a kind, gentle lady and had a beautiful cat named Dougal. Her brother had recently died, and she decided to let the rooms to help financially. She would charge us fifteen shillings a week. In those days curates in our circumstances had to pay their own rent unless the church could afford otherwise. We agreed to take the rooms and moved in. We grew very fond of Kathleen, but wondered what she would say when I told her I was having a baby. After coming home from the surgery, I went downstairs to tell her. "Yes I know," she said, "I am so pleased." "How could you possibly know?" I said. "I have only just had it confirmed by the doctor." "The neighbours told me," was her reply. How did they know? The mind boggles!

Our son Martin Hugh was born on the 26th March 1952. He had lots of dark hair and the promise of brown eyes. Kathleen became very fond of him, and told me he had helped her to cope with the loss of her brother. Before he was born, she was able to give us another room making our accommodation an upstairs flat, but we still had to go down a back staircase to the outside toilet. Because of this, and the lack of bathroom, I had to have my baby in hospital. . We were so happy, we were a family, and were rich in the things that mattered most. While I was in hospital my milk supply was so good, I had to express. One evening, coming up in the lift, a well-dressed man, obviously Jewish, said to Hugh, " My wife and I are so grateful to your wife because her milk is feeding our son." He had been born the same day as Martin and weighed only two pounds and two and a half ounces. For some reason the mother would never be able to carry full term. We left the hospital on the same day. They, in their posh car, leaving their son in the ward; we, in a rarely afforded taxi, but with our precious healthy boy.

There are always some people that are special; we would say that of Jack and Betty. With no children of their own, they were very much involved in the work of St Mary's. Jack was a Special Police Inspector and a very practically minded churchwarden. Betty sang in the choir and had a lovely voice.

I was in the vicarage one morning and noticed a big meat dish on the kitchen table piled high with delicious looking doughnuts. "Who will be consuming that lot?" I asked Daisy Collins. "The Youth Club!" she replied with a laugh. "They love their doughnuts and a cup of tea, Betty has a standing order with the baker and collects them every week."

Jack, with Hugh's help, ran the youth club, he was good with young people, they needed a firm hand, but his work as a Special Police Inspector gave him authority and the young people liked him. They came from far and wide; the news was passed around that St Mary's had a good youth club. Their main activities were playing records, table tennis and showing off their motorbikes. They were surprised that Hugh could beat them at table tennis. They would dodge the epilogue if they could, but tea and doughnuts were always a great pull!

Cecil, Hugh and Jack met each Saturday morning and tackled some of the many jobs that needed doing around the church and church hall. Some windows in the hall still had blackout paper stuck all over them, and this was five years after the war. The inner doors, leading into the main body of the church were covered with heavily studded leather. It was breaking off, looked awful, and gave a bad impression to newcomers to the church. A major repair job was undertaken, and everyone was pleased with the result.

We learned at St Mary's that in a downtown parish, if you wanted a job doing, it was best to do it yourself. The Vicar started a railings fund. Compensation paid by the Government for the railings requisitioned early in the war hardly covered the cost of the paint. New railings were eventually erected around the church site and many people got busy with a paintbrush. What a difference this made to the whole area. I noticed Cecil never asked Hugh to do something he was not prepared to do himself.

Most afternoons were taken up with visiting. The local District Nurse (a Ranyard Nurse) came to church and kept the vicar well informed of anyone needing a visit. Here is an example.

Mrs Gwynne was bedridden with elephantiasis. She cooked all her food on a Primus stove by her bed. In spite of her difficulties she was a cheerful lady and always appreciated a visit. The key was on a string, hanging behind the letterbox. Callers put a hand through the letter box, pulled the key through, unlocked the door, and calling out their names, walked down the passageway to her room. She had recently let some rooms in exchange for help with various chores. She even did her washing from her bed. A remarkable old lady!

One Christmas day, Cecil was sitting down after his Christmas dinner, ready for a well-earned rest. It was a dull day and the light was fading. He had a strong feeling that he should go and see Mrs Gwynne. Getting his bike out he cycled round to her house. Letting himself in at the front door, he called out, "It's the Vicar Mrs Gwynne, is everything alright?" "The electric meter has run out.," she replied, "and I'm left in the dark." Putting a coin in the meter he went over to see the old lady. She was lying in bed, tears in her eyes. She said, "I'm so pleased to see you, Vicar, I thought I would have to spend the rest of Christmas day in the dark. My lodgers forgot to put a shilling in the meter before they went out."

It's the small things that matter. The last straw that breaks the camel's back. Mrs Gwynne had lived her life from her bed for years. No grumbles, just gratitude for the District Nurse and friends who popped in to see her. But to be on her own, in bed, in the dark, on Christmas day was too much. The last straw! Telling me about this later Cecil said, "I know God gave me that strong urge to visit Mrs Gwynne." Because somebody cared, Mrs Gwynne cried. But God knew and He cared. And Cecil cared.

It was time to think about a move. It is hard saying goodbye. All one's feelings come to the top and you realise just how much you have come to love those you are about to leave. Love and fellowship in the Gospel can be very strong.

The Vicar of Felixstowe, Frank Howell, invited Hugh to consider a second curacy in his East Coast parish. The move would be expensive and we had no savings. What could we do? What mattered most to me was my family. I said to Hugh, "I could sell my engagement ring." He was not keen on the idea, but we both realised it was the only way we could raise money ourselves, apart from my wedding ring, and that we would never sell. We did not tell our families how hard up we were. That was between us and God and we were content to leave it that way.

We visited my parents and my brother John was there. We were talking about the move, when suddenly John looked straight at me and said, "How are you paying the removal fees?" I said, "We are OK. it's all in hand." He looked at me, shook his head, and smiling said, "No, you are not selling your engagement ring, I'll pay the bill." We gratefully accepted his offer. Even now, many years after, I look at my ring and say, "Thank you, John."

When we first went to Felixstowe to meet the vicar and look at the parish. Frank Howell was pleased to tell us there was a house to let, opposite the daughter church, St Andrew's. We saw it from the outside and were so excited. This would be our first home with a garden and Hugh said he would have a go at growing vegetables. We liked what we saw of the parish, a complete contrast to St Mary's Summerstown. Sadly, a few weeks later, we had a letter from the vicar to say that the owner of the house had died, and the house, being part of his estate, would have to be sold. Once again we would not have a home to move into, but this time we had a ten-month-old baby to complicate things. As we talked and prayed this over, we knew our faith was being tested. Hugh was sure Felixstowe was the right place for his next curacy, and we agreed that we should ago ahead, trusting our heavenly Father for the provision of a home. Frank Howell was delighted with our reply and started

17

looking around for accommodation. The only possibility was a guesthouse run by the Christian Alliance of Women and Girls.

As it was out of season they were willing to store our furniture and offer us a large living room and bedroom. Praise God, this plan worked! The staff were so helpful, and took great care of us and Martin was much loved. In a way I was on holiday and enjoyed the break from running a home, this could only be a temporary solution to the problem, but we were learning to go one step at a time.

It seems strange to say this, but the East Coast floods of 1953 came to our rescue. One end of Felixstowe is on low ground, but the part where we lived, was on high ground. During the night of January 31st a combination of high tides and east winds caused extensive flooding. The sea came up the roads, everything in its path was flooded, houses, shops, a Baptist Church. It was an area of complete devastation. Tragically people and animals were drowned. We cannot remember the exact number, but between ten and twenty folk lost their lives that night. Yet even in such sad circumstances there was another side. One old man lived in a boat on the beach at Felixstowe Ferry. It was like a big rowing boat, with a roof and chimney, I cannot remember if it had windows. He was one of the characters of Felixstowe. The night of the storm he was swept out to sea and everyone thought he had drowned. A few days later he was swept back, the local inhabitants were so pleased to see him again, safe and sound after his terrifying ordeal. Because of the flooding many families had to leave their homes and there was talk of requisitioning empty property for their use. How would we fare now?

The vicar phoned to say that a lady, who owned a small house in the parish, wanted to find tenants of her own choice. She had heard that the curate was in need of accommodation and was willing to rent the house to him, if he was interested. So very thankfully we moved into a dear little house called "Winton" and there was St Andrew's, the daughter church, at the end of the road!

18

We had been in "Winton" a few days; our furniture fitted in so well. One of the things that gave us great pleasure was locking our own front door at night, silly really, because now we take it for granted. I had cleaned the bathroom and said to Hugh, "I'll have a bath tonight." I have always enjoyed relaxing in a bath. Once Martin was in bed, we went up to the bathroom and Hugh got the gas geyser going. He was, and still is, particular about getting such things properly started and this was a large and old model. With the water running I got ready for a long relaxing bath. Hugh went out, fortunately not closing the door completely. A little later he called up to check that all was well. No answer! He came running upstairs and even before he got to the bathroom could smell gas. He ran in and said, "Get out", but I did not want to. He pulled the plug out and opened the window. By this time I was standing wrapped in a bath-towel. Bending down, Hugh looked up into the geyser and was alarmed to see something blocking the air vents, putting his arm up he started to pull and found the whole thing stuffed with rags. As they did not show, we had no idea of the problem, until the geyser was lit. The previous tenants, two elderly ladies, could not have used the geyser for years and must have taken this drastic step to prevent draughts coming down the vents and into the bathroom. The Lord certainly took care of me that night. In our prayers we both said, "Thank you Lord."

Felixstowe was totally different from Summerstown. To begin with, the pace was slower. In those days there was not much traffic, people used bicycles. The town bus, owned and driven by a Mr Aldous, was a familiar sight. One day some friends were in the bus and noticed he was stopping only if people wanted to get off, not at all the regular stops, - they were making record time. Someone called out, "What's the hurry Aldous?" He answered, "I've got fish and chips here for our supper tonight, and I want to get them home hot!" Can you imagine a London bus driver doing that!

Felixstowe was a small town then. It was a friendly, happy place where folk knew each other. We enjoyed the atmosphere and grew to love the people. The churchmanship was staunchly Protestant and evangelical, with a great missionary tradition. We discovered many different prayer groups. One we had not come across before was the "One by One Band." A group of people prayed for the same person each day, until they were converted. And it worked! My memory of Felixstowe is of a church where people prayed, expected answers, and then thanked God when He answered their prayers.

Granny Turner was another great character. Because of poor circulation she always wore Eskimo boots; they were very warm, came right up to her knees, very colourful and all leather, and would never wear out. As a young widow she had brought up three sons. Ted now sang in the parish church choir and worked for the Post Office. Arthur and Jack were pioneer missionaries in the Arctic with the Bible Churchmen's Missionary Society, (now called Crosslinks). Their story is worth repeating and I cannot do better than quote from Dr. Farrant Russell's reference to them in his book, 'Full Fifty Years', a summary of BCMS achievement up to 1972.

"Baffin Land will long remember the Turner brothers ... For twenty-five years Canon and Mrs Arthur Turner gave their lives to the Arctic. At Pangnirtung he lies amongst the people he loved ..."

" A seeming tragedy, Jack Turner's passing was to hold the attention of the world. On September 24th, 1947, as he helped a young Eskimo girl up the steps of his home with a heavy bucket of ice, the rifle under his arm slipped and went off; Jack fell, with a bullet in his brain. His wife Joan, a trained nurse, cared for him until help could be summoned. The news was sent to the outside world by motorboat and radio. The Canadian Army and Air Force set out to rescue the gravely wounded man."

"But it was not until October 4th that a parachute team was able to drop into that dangerous and little-known area, 1700 miles north of their base. The radio was smashed in the drop, and wild storms and adverse ice conditions all combined to hinder evacuation. At long last, the Dakota was able to take off from a frozen lake twenty-three miles from Moffet Inlet, the Turners' home. To the lake, the paralysed invalid had made his last journey by dog sledge. After so grim a journey, he was borne into the General Hospital in Winnipeg. And there, in spite of all that skill and devotion could do, on December 9th, John Turner passed to his reward."

On either side of the chancel of Felixstowe parish church are memorials to these ordinary, but heroic servants of the Lord Jesus Christ. The memory of their devoted mother, Granny Turner, is also very precious to us

Betty Bradley was a teacher in Ipswich and lived with Granny Turner. Nine-o-clock was bedtime for many Felixstowe folk as they were up early. One day Granny Turner said to Betty, "I always know where you are when you go out at night. If you are not in by nine-o-clock you are either with the Hydes or the Hulberts." What a reputation for the curate!

George and Florence Hyde were from London. George was a local optician. They had a daughter Deidre, born exactly a year before Martin, and a son, Robert, born while we were there in Felixstowe. We have kept in touch and visited them in their little cottage in Cullompton, Devon recently. The years have brought their changes, but we are still the same good friends, and are still thanking God for His blessing upon us and our families through the years.

Our second son Paul James was born on Sunday, 21st. February 1954. The previous Sunday, at doctor's suggestion, Hugh took the day off - I took a bottle of castor oil! We waited for things to happen, but Paul decided to wait until the following Sunday and was born at 2.15 pm just in time for a cup of tea!

Hugh took the morning service, in which he actually prayed the Litany prayer, "For all women labouring of child!" Kathleen, a teacher at the Grammar School, came round to help. She took care of Martin and finished preparing and cooking the dinner. Hugh went to a neighbour's house to phone for the doctor. It was a party line and he heard a lady chatting with a friend. "I think the Hulberts' baby is coming, the district nurse has been there most of the morning." How right she was!

Like Martin, Paul had a mass of dark hair, the promise of brown eyes, and was a happy, contented baby. Martin loved him and helped me take care of his baby brother. The following Christmas Day, for instance, on taking Paul out of his cot, I saw biscuit crumbs everywhere. Martin had shared with him the edible contents of his stocking!

While expecting Paul I had said to Hugh, "I hope I will love the new baby as much as I love Martin." As far as I could see, this thing called love was being stretched, could it stand the pressure of loving another baby? What a question! Seeing Paul was the answer. He was wonderful, an exceptionally loving baby, and still has the qualities that make people love him. Martin was a happy, lively two-year-old. I loved them both so much, but I loved them for themselves. From then on I knew there was no end to love. "Love never fails", and in Jesus love is a foretaste of eternity. It's so simple. I love Jesus and trust Him to meet every need I have on earth and for eternity. But the wonder is that He loves me!

Hugh was happy in his second curacy, I was happy as the curate's wife. Life could have gone on forever in such a place, but it was not to be. The Bishop of Barking, Hugh Gough, wrote to offer Hugh the post of minister of a new church with its own ecclesiastical district, St James', at Collier Row, on the outskirts of Romford in Essex.

CHAPTER 3
STARTING FROM SCRATCH

St James's was still being built when we first saw it. A new ecclesiastical district was formed with areas from three existing parishes. A dual-purpose church was built, with the intention of erecting a new parish church on the site later on. Hugh reminded me that we had looked out in this direction from the top of St Paul's on the day we got engaged.

Hugh became the first Minister-in-Charge. His initial task was to go to the local shopping parade and buy dustpan and brush, broom, bucket and cleaning materials and get to work cleaning up after the workmen had left. There was no band of ladies doing church cleaning; Hugh really was starting from scratch! He put out a notice, "Next Sunday. Sunday School at 3 pm, Evening Service at 6.30 pm" and waited to see what would happen. So began the work of St James's, Collier Row, Romford, Essex.

While still at Felixstowe, we received a letter from a young man, Geoff. He was a licensed lay reader in the Chichester diocese, and was marrying a young schoolteacher, Shirley, later in the year. They had written to the Bishop of Barking, Hugh Gough, asking if he knew of any churches in the Chelmsford Diocese that could do with help. Unusual, even for committed Christians I fear, they were seeking the right church, even before going to estate agents. They went to see the Bishop, and after talking things over with them, he explained the need at Collier Row, and gave them our address.

They came to see us at Felixstowe and we "clicked" right from the start. They loved the boys and fitted in so well with us, we knew we would work together and be friends. God was certainly in control of this work, right from the very beginning. Without their enthusiasm and encouragement we know the Sunday School would never have taken off as it did. The first Sunday seventy children turned up, the next, one hundred and twenty, and in four weeks we were running out of space. People

23

offered their help and Geoff was made superintendent. He arranged a system of moving chairs into straight lines for the opening period of Sunday School, into circles around the teachers for the lesson, and back into straight lines at the end - and it worked. Without his leadership things would have been in utter chaos. Geoff edited a Sunday School booklet of prayers, hymns and choruses, a fine children's introduction to Anglican worship. Later some ladies from the Women's Fellowship asked for a copy, and when she had read it, my mother said, "Please may I have one?" I know that booklet was a great blessing to her to the end of her days. Geoff was also lay reader and treasurer, his wife Shirley taught in the Sunday School at first, and later took the girl Pathfinders. She also helped me with the young wives' group and was elected on to the PCC. They found the right home too, just inside the parish boundary, and there they brought up their lovely family of two boys and two girls, Geoff has since gone to be with his Lord, a gracious, loving, gifted man, we thank God for every remembrance of him. Their eldest son, Andrew, is now in the ordained ministry.

The Diocese was negotiating for the purchase of a vicarage, some little way from the church. When we saw it we were thrilled, it was not too big and had a good garden. As things were going, we should have been in before the work began at St James, but this was not to be, the owners were held up by a "broken chain", and we could not move in until a month or so after Hugh's licensing. Housing was certainly one of the problems we had to cope with in our early days in the ministry.

At the first evening service a young couple, Kathleen and Arthur, members of the Good Shepherd church nearby, who lived across the road, offered to put Hugh up. This was a great help, as until then, he had been staying with the vicar and his wife from the Good Shepherd parish. Just before the church was finished, Kathleen and Arthur's little daughter had died from a hole in the heart. Later they had a son and eventually moved away. We lost touch, but we have always felt so grateful to them for their help, just when we needed it.

Hugh came back to Felixstowe during the week and we got ready to move, but with two young children we could not live out of boxes!

Derek was another person who came to help. He had worshipped at the Church of the Good Shepherd with his parents, but felt it was right to come to St James. He became churchwarden and was always such an encourager and absolutely dependable. Pathfinders became another sphere of his work. Later, he took over from Geoff as treasurer. God brought people to us who became our friends in the gospel, and as with Geoff and Shirley, we thank God for every remembrance of Derek. And so we could go on, with many more names of those who gave unstinting support in those early days of St James Church.

One Saturday morning Hugh was cycling up to the church and was stopped by Jean, she was a teacher, who lived and taught in Devon, but came home to her parents for the holidays. Jean was waiting for Hugh and handed him an envelope saying, "Please accept this as a gift for the work at St James's." Inside was a cheque for £500! A lot of money in 1955! Jean had had thoughts about missionary work, but for various reasons was not able to go ahead with her plans. For sometime she had been praying that a new church would be built in her home area, and felt that God was telling her to make a gift of the money she had put by originally to help with her training for overseas service. You can imagine how encouraged we were by this wonderful and unexpected gift, a lovely example of sacrificial giving. Eventually it was used for the purchase of an electronic organ to replace the old harmonium with which we had started - and very appropriately Jean's sister Janet was our first very able organist!

I started a Women's Fellowship, and we had a good group of women interested. I felt my youth with such people, I was under 30 years old, and often before the meeting would find my tummy was being silly. I had not come to terms with taking meetings and worried about it. One day Hugh gave me a very serious look, and said, in a deliberately parsonic voice, "This must stop my dear, we cannot afford the toilet paper!" Because he made me see how silly I was, and we laughed about it, I got over my Women's Fellowship nerves and realised this was very much my sphere of work, and enjoyed taking the meetings.

One person who stands out in my memory is Mrs Biggs. During the war, she was getting ready to go to her Women's meeting, where she played the piano. Her bungalow suffered a direct hit in an air raid, and her only child, a little daughter of about 2 years old was killed. Mrs Biggs woke up in hospital completely blind. As she began to realise the full extent of her injuries, and grieving over the loss of her little girl, she thought, "I must divorce my husband, I cannot have any more children now." She must have received other injuries, but her blindness was all she ever mentioned. A vicar's wife, who had two part-sighted sons, visited her, and listened to all she had to say, and then encouraged her to forget all about divorce, and make a new life for herself, and her husband, even though she was blind.

When I first met Mrs Biggs she had a son and daughter, and the family lived in a little bungalow, near the church. The only thing she could not do was go out on her own, but friends took her everywhere, she was a popular lady. Having been a good pianist before her blindness, we discovered that if we took her over to the piano, and put her finger on middle 'C' she could play any tune she remembered

One day she told me, "When I could see, I used to worry, but now I'm in darkness and cannot see, I don't worry at all. I suppose it's because I have to trust God more" Mrs Biggs was in darkness as far as her sight was concerned, but spiritually, she had more sight than most of us. A remarkable lady and one I admired greatly.

Our daughter, Ruth Mary Joy was born on 21st. January 1956, a joy from the start. She had dark hair, and like her brothers before her, the promise of dark eyes. The boys loved her and helped me take care of their baby sister. With two boisterous brothers, we thought Ruth would be a tomboy, but

26

from earliest days she had a gentle and quiet way with her. The boys loved to see her in pretty dresses and were so proud of her - I don't remember any jealousy between them, they were good friends and played well together. We were so blessed; three happy healthy children and I would never lose them in a crowd; with such dark hair and eyes they could only be mine. One point I should mention here is that before he met me, Hugh preferred blondes! When he first introduced me to his parents, they looked at me and said to each other afterwards, "He must be serious"!

Martin started school and from the beginning enjoyed it very much. He was so enthusiastic and soon fell in love with his teacher. I met a new set of mums and decided it was the time to start a "Young Wives group." This proved popular, especially as on some Sundays, Hugh would have as many as twelve baptisms and his contact with the families provided an opportunity to tell the mothers about Young Wives, and invite them along. He would go to church during Sunday school, help with getting the church ready for the evening service, take the baptisms, have his tea in the church kitchen, and then lead the worship or preach. Geoff's help, as a lay reader, made all the difference. The afternoons and evening were long for both of us. Later, we started a young people's fellowship meeting in the vicarage. I seldom got to church at night now, but we were together in all we did, in love with each other, and the God we served, and were experiencing that "Godliness with contentment is great gain."

With Martin at school, we decided on an after Easter break and because, like most little boys, Martin and Paul were fascinated by trains, we arranged a camping coach holiday near Folkestone. With all the axing of stations and services, I don't think this is still a part of the railway network but it was a good idea. A few old coaches were put in a siding, near a station, and fitted with bunks and a kitchen and sitting area, and there, one could camp in comfort. The accommodation was good, clean and comfortable and, with many trains going by, it was a perfect solution for our holiday. We used trains to get to the site and for outings, perfect for families like ours, without a car.

Many children in Martin's school had developed a persistent cough and as the holiday drew nearer, we said, "A change of air would do him good."

One of Hugh's aunts, Vera, already a favourite with the children, accepted an invitation to join us. We arrived, as usual, with everything but the kitchen sink; no matter how much we pruned the things the children must take, it was always far too much in our eyes. We got ourselves sorted out, beds made up, food put away, and then a cup of tea for us, and something to drink for the children, while we looked at the time table, and as Hugh had thought, the Golden Arrow train passed through the station every day.

The boys were really excited about sleeping on a train, Paul, now three and a quarter, said to me, his brown eyes shining with excitement, "I'm going to sleep on a brink, no a brunk, no a brank - O, what is it mummy?"

Sadly, after a few days, Martin became very unwell; I asked the stationmaster if he could tell me of a local doctor, as a visit was indicated - he said he would ring for us. The doctor came, took one look at Martin and said, "Measles - and I'm afraid the others will go down with it before long, it's highly infectious." It was agreed that we could stay until the Friday, so that the coach could be fumigated, ready to receive its next occupants. As we would not be able to travel home by train because of infection, the doctor very kindly arranged for an ambulance instead.

Our plans for some exciting excursions had to be abandoned. However while auntie Vera and I cared for the invalid and fifteen months old Ruth, Hugh did take Paul for a couple of trips. One was to the Romney, Hythe, and Dymchurch light railway, and that was great fun. As they went into a dark and gloomy village church, Paul turned to his father and said, "Daddy, is this the dim church?" When it was time for a meal he was treated to a lunch in a restaurant. Hugh returned to us still laughing at the way Paul had tucked in to a hearty meal, quite unaware that he was entertaining people with his enthusiastic enjoyment of his food, and, on this occasion at least, his excellent table manners! Thankfully, by the Friday, Martin was feeling much better, and was able to enjoy the journey back to Romford, quite proud of being responsible for our eighty-mile drive home in an ambulance!

A friend called one day and asked, with a laugh, "May I have tea and biscuits please, here is my 2d." "What are you talking about?" I asked. She replied, "The notice on your front gate." As I was still puzzled she said, "Come out and have a look." The children and I followed her out of the front door, down the garden path, to the front gate, a big five-barred gate, recently painted white. Attached to it by string was a notice, in Martin's handwriting: "Tea and biscuits 2d." Looking at me Martin said, "I thought we could make some money, we are always giving people cups of tea!" How right he was and how I wish I had kept that notice!

As Hugh reminded me, there is an update of this story, but the price of tea has gone up, and there are no biscuits!

Just under forty years later - it is now 1995 - we have Martin married to Alison, with three children, Vicki, 15 years old, David, 11 years, and Amie, 9 years. Paul and his wife Anna live in Switzerland and have Oliver, two and a half years, and Leona just coming up to one year. Ruth is married to Mark and they have Rachel 14 years old, Clare, 12 years, and Jonathan (Jonny), 10 years.

Ruth was coming up to her 40th birthday. Talking about it with Mark he said, "I wanted to give Ruth a birthday party, away from the kitchen sink and cooking!" We suggested Pilgrim Hall, a Christian Conference Centre and Hotel in East Sussex. Mark contacted family and friends, inviting them to a luncheon, followed by tea and birthday cake later.

To our amazement, 80 people booked in for the lunch. Some stayed from the evening meal on Friday to Sunday tea, others from Saturday lunch to Sunday tea; others came for lunch and tea on the Saturday.

When the "Saturday only" friends and family had gone, we were sitting around a log fire, relaxed and comfortable, and Ruth said, "This has been a perfect day, full of surprises, how you contacted so many people, I don't know, but to be greeted by Paul and Oliver, when we arrived on Friday evening, was the greatest surprise of all." Someone picked up a guitar and started playing, we got the song books out and had a time of fellowship, reminding me of our Portsmouth days when the family were still at home

When we finished singing Hugh said, "We wondered about a time of fellowship and praise tomorrow morning, followed by Holy Communion", and this was warmly received. As soon as Hugh had finished, David stood up, a large pad and pen in his hand, and said, as spokesman for Jonny, and his friend, Stephen, "We have arranged to make early morning tea and will bring it to your rooms at 7.30am. we will take your orders now, the charge is 10p. a cup"! He looked around expectantly to see who would take up their offer!

We all knew tea was free, and could be made at any time!

The boys had seen the 'Tuck shop', and being a bit short of cash, put their heads together to remedy the situation. Hugh and I gave them 10p each for showing initiative, and asked for a cup of tea right away. Others did the same. I think they did quite well on Saturday night, as well as Sunday morning! So you see it was a real case of 'like father, like son'!

The boys had sorted out their cash problem, but Amie was still in need. After our time of fellowship on Sunday morning, I went to our bedroom, probably to take my Bible back and hearing a knock at the door called out, "Come in." It was Amie, looking a little unsure of herself, as she said, "Granny, are you going to empty your purse on this holiday?" The penny dropped, Amie wanted to go to the tuck shop, but was short of ready money. She knew that when we visited them in Wimborne, not so often as Ruth's family at Reigate, because the journey is much longer, we usually stayed a few days, and I always had a lot of small change to divide between David and herself. This holiday had been far too busy to sort out my purse, but Amie had not forgotten, and I was able to make a visit to the tuck shop worthwhile. The children did not know that Pilgrim Hall had such a good tuck shop, and had not brought any pocket money.

With eight grandchildren, we try to be fair to them all, and this reminded me that Vicki, Rachel and Clare, on the basis of fairness for all, would need a contribution also to keep the books right.

But to get back to my story, having skipped nearly 40 years!

Hugh asked me if I knew where a pair of his pliers had got to, he had searched high and low, but could not find them. I had no idea where they could be, but Martin said, "I've got them in my bedroom", and ran upstairs. When he came down, Hugh asked him, "What did you want the pliers for Martin?" His explanation was so simple, "The sweet shop at the top of the road has some new Dinky cars, and my tooth is nearly out, so I've been pulling it with the pliers. I want to put the tooth under my pillow, and get the sixpence, then I'll have enough money to buy a new Dinky car."

Martin had a rabbit called Benny and when someone gave us a kitten, all black, apart from a white spot under its chin, we decided the kitten should be Paul's. He was thrilled and called it Mickey. We were assured it was a male! A few weeks later, it was time to think of getting Mickey neutered. Ruth and I went into Romford, a sixpenny bus ride then from the Collier Row terminus. We were carrying Mickey in a zip bag and took great care that he did not get out, but he was not at all impressed with the journey and made quite a noise. When it was our turn the vet examined Mickey, and said, "You will have to change the name to Michelle, bring her back later and have her spayed!" We walked to the bus stop and waited, but when it came, the bus was full up downstairs. We decided to go upstairs and I helped Ruth negotiate the curve in the stairs, not easy when the bus was on its way, with Mickey telling the world she was being badly treated. The only seat was right up at the front. We

31

eventually reached it; I put the bag under the seat and helped Ruth up. Pulling out the bag I realised the zip was undone and we were minus one kitten! We looked under the seat, no sign of Mickey anywhere. I was concerned about the stairs and had to act quickly. Standing up, and in what I would call my loud "taking meetings voice", I called out, "Could you help me? We have lost a little black kitten, she is somewhere up here, and could be under your seat. Please would you look for her?" Remember, only the able bodied could managed the winding stairs, once the bus was moving! When there is a real need I have always found people so helpful. They were all looking under their seats when someone at the back shouted out, "I've found her." Everyone was pleased as Mickey was handed back to me, a bundle of noisy, black fur, but all was well, Mickey was found, and I breathed a sigh of relief as I made sure the zip was secure, and Mickey could not get up to any more tricks. Paul got his female kitten back, but decided to keep the name of Mickey. Ruth enjoyed her trip to Romford, and Paul, probably at school, was sorry to miss the fun!

We were having tea one evening when the bell rang, Hugh got up to answer it, and I heard him take someone into the lounge, and after a while he went into the study. He came back about ten minutes later, sat down, and got on with his tea, but did not say who had called so eventually I asked, "Who was that at the front door?" Hugh gave me a blank look at first and then said, "That was David (a member of the P.C.C.) and I've left him in the lounge!" As he said this, there was a knock and David put his head round the door. "I thought you must have forgotten me," he said as Hugh apologised. I wonder what we had for tea that day, not fish I'm sure!

The work with young people was encouraging; we had a holiday on the Broads, a great success. The services were going well. A band of ladies kept the church clean. Brownies and Guides, and later Boys' Brigade were started. The women's work gave me much pleasure. We had a choir and organist. PCC members were working well together. An extension fund was launched and was well supported by Sunday school parents, people just moved into the parish who had their children baptised, as well as church members. A Bible study and prayer meeting met in the Parsonage. The magazine went into many homes. There was a lot of goodwill locally for St James's. The church was making its impact on the community and people responded.

A local man, George, had a flower stall at Romford market and started coming to church with his wife. His teenage children already belonged to the Youth Club. George became involved in a delightfully practical way. Whenever anyone from Church, this was usually one of the Young Wives, had a baby, he would take them a bunch of flowers. I had freesias when Ruth was born. People going to him for funeral flowers were often given a small tract or card, he was concerned by the sight of people grieving for their loved ones. Standing by his flower stall, dressed in his brown overalls, with his hat on the back his head, he would offer words of comfort as he sold the mourners their flowers. George was one of God's ordinary saints, selling flowers at Romford Market but with a heart of gold.

In so many ways, we saw practical Christianity shown by many caring, loving people and they enriched our lives.

The Bishop had told Hugh that five years should be the limit of his work in such a church situation. It was hard going, but we enjoyed it, and when Hugh left, he knew he would be leaving a good foundation for another man to build on. This has proved to be the case, the dual-purpose church became the new church and a new church hall was built. We went back some years ago and it was good to see that a number of those involved in the early days were still part of the church family, but obviously some of the older folk were no longer around.

Hugh's parents had moved to Bognor Regis before the war ended and we spent many happy holidays with them. The beach was about fifteen minutes walk from the house, with sands that were ideal for family picnics and play. While there one year we talked about our need for a car, for parish work and family use.

Hugh went everywhere on his bike and I walked with the children or we got the bus. We prayed and put out a fleece. If we had two hundred pounds in the bank Hugh would take driving lessons. I must state here that we had no savings at all, we were living from hand to mouth, and always waiting for the next payday. Two hundred pounds seemed two hundred years away! In no way did this worry us; we simply trusted God to meet our needs and always had enough. We left it to "Our Father" to "Give us each day our daily bread." "Take no anxious thought for tomorrow," Jesus said, "Your Father knows your needs." I have always loved that verse in Hebrews which says, "Faith is the evidence of things hoped for, the substance of things not seen." My logical mind tells me that if I cannot trust God here on earth, I cannot trust Him for heaven and eternity either.

About two days before we were due to leave Bognor, Hugh's mother received a cheque, part of a legacy from an aunt, much more than she had expected, and wonderful mother that she was, she gave each of her children two hundred pounds!

We arrived back in Romford after a good holiday all ready for work and school. Hugh opened the pile of letters awaiting his attention. The last was from CPAS, the Church Pastoral-Aid Society, asking if he would consider working as Organising Secretary in the Southwest, based at Bristol. To do this work, he must be able to drive!

Hugh had his driving lessons, but failed his first test. The second had to be at least a month later, and that would be the day before we were due to move! CPAS had supplied us with an Austin Countryman for use in Bristol, and friends went out with him. Derek, the churchwarden, said, "If you don't pass the test, I'll drive you to Bristol." We certainly had good friends; it was not easy leaving them. The great day came, I heard the car come round the corner and into the drive, Hugh gave three short blasts on the horn and I knew he had passed!

CHAPTER 4
THE WEST COUNTRY

As we arrived in Bristol, the University clock struck midnight, we were very tired, Hugh had driven all the way, and we had the cat, the dog, the rabbit and the tortoise with us in the car. Fortunately the children were staying with our families in London. Our sleeping bags were rolled out on the floor, and after we had sorted out the animals, we had a hot drink from a flask and rolled into bed. The removal men were due at nine-o-clock. At eight the doorbell rang, the men had arrived an hour before their time. They explained that they had slept in the van, but had been moved on by the police and thought they might as well start early and get the job done. Our one consolation was that they would finish early! The usual cups of tea and biscuits kept them going and us! The blessings of an electric kettle in a move cannot be overestimated, along with sufficient tea, sugar, milk and biscuits, to be used when necessary! Often, in this case! But all good things come to an end, and eventually we were on our own, and as we looked around the house we had a warm feeling inside, this was our home for the next few years, the thought pleased us and we were happy. A detached house with two large and one small bedroom, a dining room, sitting room, breakfast room and kitchen with a fair sized garden. With church, schools and shops within easy walking distance, what more could one ask?

The question brought the answer - food: we were very hungry. We did not know the area well, but had been told where to find the shops, and so we walked to what was to be my new shopping centre and found a restaurant open and ordered the most delicious omelette, with bread and butter and a pot of tea. We felt at home and liked all we saw. I enjoyed the stone pavements, so different to the ones in Romford, they did not glitter in the sun, and had a timelessness about them, the same went for so many of the houses, and although ours was only about thirty years old, it fitted in well with the rest. We knew the children would be thrilled with their new home and, bless them, they were. Martin was 7, Paul 5 and Ruth 3, our children, how we thanked God for them, and prayed for them daily, as we still do, together with their families. We know the strength of a Christian family has many facets, one is prayer, others are, love, friendship and togetherness, honesty and truthfulness, the list is as endless as God's endless love. St.Paul hits the nail right on the head in 1 Corinthians 13, when he writes, "But the greatest of these is love."

Hugh was soon busy in the study, planning his work for CPAS in the south western dioceses from Gloucester to Salisbury and westwards to Truro. I contacted the local church school which Martin and Paul would attend right away and Ruth later on. We went to Redland Church without Hugh. He was away taking meetings, during the week, and preaching on Sundays, in the parishes linked with CPAS. The children attended Sunday School and I got involved with the Women's Meeting and a Bible study group. I enjoyed being one of the congregation with no responsibilities, this gave me a freedom in my family life that is not always possible in a vicarage. We got to know our neighbours and church friends, in some ways our life style had changed, but we both believed it was good for us as a family.

We decided to get a television as I was on my own so much, especially at night. "Dixon of Dock Green" and "Dr. Who" became firm favourites with the boys. Ruth did not appreciate "Dr Who", and hid behind the settee if anything scary came on the screen, but she enjoyed the children's afternoon programmes, we watched them together, before going to meet the boys from school.

About this time Pamela Ragbourne came into our family life. Working for CPAS, she co-ordinated the women's side of the work, in those days known as "The Ladies Home Mission Union." Later the name was changed to "Women's Action." Pam fitted in so well with our family, always the acid test, and during Paul's illness was supportive and helpful in many ways. Again and again people come into our lives, just when we needed

36

them, we saw God's hand in this. The first book of Samuel chapter 25, part of verse 29, uses a delightful phrase, Abigail says to David, "The life of my master will be bound securely in the bundle of the living by the Lord your God." Even if we part and meet again, sometimes years later, we take up where we left off, because God in His love for us ties His, "bundles of the living" with the cords of love.

We had only been in Bristol about six weeks when Paul said his legs hurt, we thought it was because we had to walk up or down hill to go anywhere from our front door. Bristol is said to be, like Rome, a city built on seven hills and we were proving this to be true. A few days later, he was unwell and I sent for doctor. After examining Paul he said, "He has got either polio or rheumatic fever." He was not sure, and needed to do tests. We were devastated. Paul was not running a high temperature, but was ill and we knew something was wrong. Hugh was due to be away for the weekend and went off very heavy-hearted, leaving me with the telephone number of the vicarage he was to visit. The doctor rang later and said Paul had rheumatic fever, there was no doubt, but he had a friend staying with him, a heart specialist, and he would like to bring him round to see Paul on Monday. Of course I said yes.

That was a very hard, lonely weekend. Inside I was crying, "No God, this cannot be true, not Paul", but I had to keep up appearances for Martin and Ruth's sake, and Paul needed me. I rang our vicar, Richard Higginson and asked for prayer. The only thing I could thank God for was the visit of our doctor's friend on Monday and the loving support of friends as they were told our news.

Hugh arrived back home, and we tried to concentrate on doing things until the doctors' visit that afternoon. When they arrived we took them upstairs and they chatted to Paul. The specialist put a wooden case on a chair, and said to Paul, "I want to see what is happening inside you and this case will help me." Getting Paul's interest, the doctor gave him an Electro-Cardiogram in bed. The result of the tests was that he wanted

Paul to spend one month in bed and to be on penicillin for two years. He raised the question of Paul going into hospital. A loud "No" came from Paul and myself and our doctor agreed to see his young patient daily, if I took and recorded his temperature night and morning ready for his visit.

After a few days on penicillin I noticed Paul's tongue was getting black and mentioned this to doctor; he thought for a moment and said, "MacIntosh toffees are the answer, give Paul one three times a day, that will clear his tongue." And they did, much to Paul's delight. He had his tin of toffees by the bed and shared them with his brother and sister; probably one three times a day, so everyone was happy!

Paul was off school for about three months. I began to hear of other children with the same illness and felt we had got off very lightly, and were so thankful for the help and support of our doctor. Gradually Paul got better, but could not rush around like other boys at first. However he became interested in chess and from an early age seemed to know his way around the board. (Today he has programmed his computer to play chess!) Hugh's father came to visit us and bought his grandson a book on chess, and played many games with him. Grandad was a teacher, a keen chess player, and as a mathematician, had started a chess club at his school. On retirement he was given a pendulum clock, with a loud strike, we have it now in our hall, but don't wind the striker. We did at first, but prefer a quieter life, especially in the early hours of the morning! Of course Martin became involved in chess too, and would often play a game with his brother. I should mention here that Hugh also enjoys chess and in retirement has time for the monthly "Tough Puzzles" magazine. We enjoy "Countdown", the words and numbers game on channel 4, and usually watch it while having a cup of tea and one of Hugh's homemade ginger biscuits.

Six months after the onset of his illness, Paul went to hospital for a checkup. By this time he was looking well and enjoying school again and was more or less back to normal. Another Electro-Cardiograph revealed that all was well. When I went to doctor for the outcome of the hospital visit, he read out the letter to me, saying that Paul could live a normal unrestricted life. Our precious son was well, we were so fortunate and could only praise and thank God. One thing doctor mentioned though was that if Paul should ever need a tooth extraction, it was advisable for him to have penicillin. Sometime later an extraction did become necessary so once again we went to see doctor. He was so kind and explained this entailed an injection with a rather big needle, and if we went in a few days time, he would give the injection. We went at the appropriate time, Paul was a bit apprehensive, but doctor said he knew how brave he would be. Looking up at a case full of books our son said, "I will be brave if you give me one of your green books", and pointed to the great big volumes of a medical dictionary! Doctor got up, went to the bookcase, picked one out, put it on his desk and said to Paul, "You can take that home with you after the injection." Paul never made a sound and left the surgery with the book under his arm. It was heavy though, and I had to carry it most of the way home. Paul was so proud of his book and used it for years as a doorstop for his bedroom door! I don't think he ever read it, I certainly did not!

We have so much to thank Doctor Pyke for. I don't think he is alive now, but he was a good doctor and a man with a great understanding of children. The National Health Service should be proud to employ such men. They are born doctors, as well as being trained as doctors. As patients, we soon know what sort of GP, or consultant, we are dealing with, the born and trained or just trained, and I know which I prefer!

At four Ruth was like my shadow, always involved with whatever I was doing and chatting away merrily all the time. She had a way of saying things back to front, and with her attractive childish lisp, could have us guessing at times. One day, I was ironing the boys' shirts, Ruth left whatever she was doing and came over to me and said, "God overalls are churtz." I could not believe my ears and asked, "What did you say dear?" Out it came again, "God overalls are churtz." Was she trying to say, "God overrules our Church"? I looked at my four- year-old daughter and thought, "I know her father is a clergyman, but this is deep theology, far beyond the knowledge of a child as young as this!" I had left my ironing by this time and was really concentrating on every word she said. I asked, "Please will you say that again, dear, I don't understand." Ruth looked a little cross and repeated: "God overalls are churtz." Obviously I was the dumb one, she knew exactly what she was saying! I knelt down and asked her to repeat each word slowly, so she pointed to the shirt and said again, "God overalls are churtz." None the wiser, I said, "Yes, dear." She smiled and said, "Churtz make God overalls." Then the penny dropped. "Shirts make good overalls", or "Good overalls are shirts", whatever way round; it was the same thing to Ruth. The boys had been told at school that their old shirts would make good overalls for painting or any dirty work. Ruth had simply been reminding me of this! We finished the ironing and went to meet the boys. I felt relieved that we had not got a religious child prodigy on our hands, but a normal, happy daughter, who sometimes said things back to front.

While we were at Bristol, Martin started to show an interest in photography. I was collecting Paul's tablets from the chemist. The children stayed outside, but I could see Martin's school cap through the goods in the window, something had obviously got his interest. The shop assistant said, "We often see that young boy looking through the window, he seems to be fascinated by the camera, he came and asked for a leaflet, but just stands and looks and then goes away, we've all noticed him at times." I went out to see what was so special about the camera and discovered my son was quite knowledgeable about it, and would like to buy it, the only problem was the price. I knew he was saving up and enjoyed Christmas and birthdays because he was often given money as a present to spend as he wished. We talked about the camera and his savings and I realised he had a long way to go before he could buy it, but he saved all he could and eventually went into the shop and bought his first camera. He entered a competition for children, in the Church of England Newspaper, and won a prize with his holiday picture of a sailing boat on the Norfolk Broads, I think the prize was seven shillings and six pence, his first payment for taking a photograph. He was thrilled and so were we. I have asked Martin to design the cover of this book and am so happy that he has agreed to do so.

Hugh was enjoying his work, especially his contact with the clergy, and realised some men could miss out on fellowship, feeling lonely and cut off from friends, they lived in such way-out places and some roads were not too good in those days. At times he got lecturers and students from Tyndale Hall or Clifton Theological College to go with him, preaching in one church in the morning and another at night, but he was always the visiting preacher and missed the pastoral aspect of parish work. We began to realise that our time at Bristol was coming to an end. Martin was now coming up to eleven, and would soon be sitting his eleven plus exam, not the best time to change counties and schools. Paul was nine, and Ruth seven, it would be easy to move them as far as schooling was concerned, but where?

A letter arrived from our friend, Don Churchman, who was Vicar of St Jude's, Southsea, telling Hugh about St Luke's, a neighbouring parish. They needed a vicar, but it was a run down area, due for a lot of demolition and then rebuilding. With Martin sitting his eleven plus examination in a few months, we felt that to change his school at such a time was not a good idea. In any case we were not convinced it was the right place. Hugh wrote back thanking Don but saying it was not for us, and we forgot all about it.

Of course we continued to pray about the future, and wanted to be sure that we would find the place of God's appointment. Then another letter about St Luke's, Southsea, arrived! But this one was from the Bishop of Portsmouth, asking if Hugh would come and talk the matter over with him. Hugh was due to be at a CPAS staff conference at Mabledon over the new

41

year period, 1963, and had planned to spend a night with his parents at Bognor on the return journey. A visit to Portsmouth could be fitted in easily. To our surprise we both now believed that this could after all be our next sphere of service. The Bishop's secretary was contacted and an appointment arranged.

Hugh enjoyed the conference as he always did, a great time of fellowship with other CPAS representatives from around the country and with the head office staff too. He tells me that one of his memories, probably of an earlier occasion, is of going down to the lounge at Mabledon well before breakfast to tune into a Test Match broadcast from Australia - and finding Dick Lucas, of St Helen's, Bishopsgate fame, already well informed as to England's progress!

The journey home from Kent, via Sussex and Hampshire, had to be made over snow-covered roads, but was successfully undertaken. The Bishop was very frank about the challenge that St Luke's would bring, but also stressed the opportunities provided by its central situation and the fact that alongside was the largest church school in the diocese. The next step would be for Hugh to bring me to meet the churchwardens and see the vicarage and church and then let him know if we were prepared to go further.

We made our visit a few weeks later - still the big freeze up and some roads impassable, so the journey had to be made by train. We remember the all-white landscape of Salisbury Plain! We soon saw that it would not be an easy parish, things were at a very low ebb and the whole area looked so miserable. There was a large Victorian vicarage, the busy Portsmouth and Southsea station was just across the road, and nearby were a number of refrigeration plants for a meat market. Later we were to discover that these became active at five o'clock in the morning! There was one consolation, the Guildhall clock was then visible from all the front rooms, and we could sit up in bed and tell the time! With no central heating, and poor decoration, we had to be quite sure that this was God's choice of a home for the children and us. Don and Mary Churchman kindly put us up overnight at St Jude's Vicarage and talked and prayed with us about the situation. They confirmed that the children would be able to attend their church junior school until they were old enough for grammar school.

We returned to Bristol aware that a difficult decision had to be made affecting the whole family. We remembered our covenant with God to go wherever He wanted us. We remembered we had stopped once on Portsdown Hill on a journey from Bognor to Bristol and had looked out over the parishes of Portsea Island wondering if we would ever be called to minister there. It seemed that the Lord was giving us a strong feeling that this was the right place for the next few years no matter how hard the task might be. We wrote to the Bishop, and he formally offered the living and hoped we would be able to start at St Luke's before Easter.

The Diocese was very short of money for any decoration or work to the vicarage. With its dark brown doors, and grey paint for the rest of the woodwork, we wondered if a former vicar had been friendly with the captain of a battleship! The ceilings were high, the rooms big, with long corridors, and it looked gloomy and neglected. I measured the curtains and saw some of the windows did not have curtain rails, another problem, and we needed well over a 100 yards of 48 inch material, without allowing for pelmets, and that was skimping things, and it would take hours to measure and make the curtains. As for carpets, they were almost a non-starter. The vicarage had not been lived in for over a year, it was cold and needed a good clean. We did what we always do in such situations, we prayed.

With the move in mind, and realising we would soon be living in a big house, Martin, who by now had passed his eleven plus exam, put his thinking cap on, and decided to do something about our need for more furniture. The children came home for lunch each day, and one Friday, Martin followed me out to the van when the greengrocer called for my order. I went back into the house, probably for my purse, and came back to see

Martin and the man having quite a conversation. They had a wooden orange box, on its end, standing in the road, and as I watched, Martin picked the box up and proudly carried it into the house. Our greengrocer friend was so amused: Martin had explained our need and asked if he had any wooden boxes, as he wanted to make some furniture. Together they had decided that the orange box would make a good bedside table. On its end, varnished, with 'Contact' of his choice, on the top and middle shelf, (and some help from Dad) Martin's bedside table was by his bed until he left home to get married!

We got organised for our move and all went to the dentist for a final check up. Coming home, Martin ran ahead to one of his favourite shops, where they displayed a notice board advertising articles for sale. He came running back to me, very excited, saying, "A house near us is selling some long curtains, and they are cheap." I looked at the notice, knowing we had little spare cash at the time, but we had got half an answer to our prayer, we knew where to buy some long curtains, and they were cheap at £4 a pair. Hugh's sister Pen was staying with us and was amused at the way we all got involved with our need for curtains.

Hugh was on his way home from a Hampshire parish, but decided to make a detour, and call on his parents in Bognor. He also called on two of his aunts. One of them said, "I'm so pleased you have called, I was going to put this in the post, to help with your move, but you might as well take it now", and she handed him a cheque for a hundred pounds. He arrived home that night, and told us about the cheque, we told him about the curtains! Later Pen and I went to the house, and bought almost enough curtains for the Portsmouth Vicarage with that one hundred pounds, and of course, there was a good amount left over. They were beautifully made, most in velvet or brocade material, and at £4 a pair, were just right for our needs. "Jehovah-Jireh, the Lord will provide." We have proved this again and again, and some of you reading this book, can say the same. Praise the Lord. Martin chose a plush plum coloured pair for his bedroom. When he married and moved away, I asked if he would like his curtains, knowing he would, and today he still uses them as curtains for the front door. I had them cleaned before giving them to him. When I collected them the assistant asked, "Are they from a church, they are such a rich colour and a very unusual material?"

Leaving the work of the Church Pastoral-Aid Society was just like saying goodbye to a family. The prayer input from the London staff was so encouraging, and they were so supportive during Paul's illness, we knew we would miss them. The General Secretary, Canon Mohan was a most gracious and caring man, and Jimmy Cotton, the accountant was so enthusiastic and with his ready smile and encouraging words, a man of God, who used his talents willingly in his Master's service. We knew our contact with CPAS would continue, but that we would be on the receiving end, one of the many parishes in need of help, mostly financial. This proved to be so true, many of our children from St Luke's went to their summer camps. Later Patsy Jenks, our Parish Worker (since ordained) and Robert, one of our young people, and still today a member of our extended family, helped with the camps, so that we were able to give as well as receive.

CHAPTER 5
ALL CHANGE AT ST LUKE'S

Hugh was instituted as Vicar of St Luke's, Southsea, on Maundy Thursday, in the year 1963. The Church was full and I thought, "We seem to have a good congregation here." But on Easter Sunday it was a different story, I remember feeling so let down, where were the people? But we did meet church members who would give us wonderful help and encouragement in the years to come, and we thanked God for them.

The vicarage presented many problems, everything needed attention at once, but we had beds and curtains, and some carpets. The dining room had been redecorated and was the first room ready to receive visitors. We were surprised at the numbers of tramps, men of the road, just passing through, who knocked and asked for food and drink, and sometimes money, which we rarely gave. Many were from prison, some from the Isle of Wight. As soon as they saw our curtains up, the doorbell started. "Could you give me the price of a cup of tea and a sandwich, I haven't any money." I started giving tea and cheese sandwiches. The news got round and we were inundated. We did not allow the children to answer the door at this time. I always bought at least an extra pound of cheese and put two mugs and a spoon under the kitchen sink and called them "tramps' cups." No one else used them, only the men of the road.

Eventually, we got to know some of them; one I called Charlie was quite a character. In the winter, he left a trail of newspaper wherever he went, and as I let him eat and drink in the porch, there was usually a pile of screwed up paper on the floor where he had been standing. I discovered later that he was known locally as "Paper Jack"! He always started his conversation to me with, "Hey, Missus". When he got to know me better the "Hey, Missus" was followed by "Have you got a cap?" or another time, "Hey, Missus, have you got a coat?" or "Hey, Missus, I've banged my head, have you got some embrocation?" But the best one of all was when he said, "Hey, Missus, have you got some trousers?" Taking the short cut through the station forecourt one day, I spotted Charlie, looking in the rubbish bins, and thought he had not noticed me, but he had, and called out, "Hey, Missus, I'll be round to see you soon."

I was in the vicarage on my own one day when Charlie called; it was just tea and sandwiches this time. The local undertaker rang and as dealing with him would take time, I said, "Could I ring you later, I've got Charlie on the doorstep", and put the phone down. To my surprise, a few minutes later the undertaker came in at the front gate, while I was still dealing with Charlie. "Can I speak to you for a moment?" he said. We went into the study. He asked, "Are you alone here?" I answered, "I am, the Vicar is out, but the children will soon be home from school. Why are you so concerned that I'm on my own with Charlie?" He said, "He has a bad reputation locally, and has terrified my own wife so much, she is afraid to answer the door to him. He is abusive and his language is foul. I thought that if you were on your own you might need help." I was grateful for his concern for me, but as he could see, I did not have problems with Paper Jack. This puzzled both of us. Hugh came in and my friend explained what he was doing in the study, and Hugh thanked him for his help. He told us Charlie had property and quite a bit of money, but chose to live the way he did.

Next time he called I took a good look at his face and saw that underneath the beard and dirt, he had a fine face. He had never sworn at me, or been abusive in any way, he just said, "Hey Missus, can I have ...?" I wondered what had gone wrong in Charlie's life; he could have been such a different man. We sometimes gave tracts, and asked the men to read them later, in the hope that something would get through, but they were often thrown down outside the gate. I don't know the answer to this problem, apart from Jesus, but they would not give Him a chance. Maybe it's not such a disturbing factor of vicarage life now, but my heart would ache for these men, as it did for Charlie.

Jesus said, "Come unto to me all you who are troubled and heavy laden and I will give you rest." But He also said, "And they would not."

We had been in the vicarage about a month, and it was beginning to feel more like home. On the evening I have in mind, Hugh was in the lounge, getting rid of some of the battleship grey and dark brown paint, that gave the vicarage such a heavy, dull gloomy look, but once up the ladder, he did not want to come down, until he was ready to paint the next bit. As I've said, the ceilings were so very high, and fortunately, someone had given us a long ladder they no longer had use for. The children were in bed, we had long since had our evening meal, but for some reason we were both hungry, and when I mentioned fish and chips to Hugh, he said, "Yes please, but I don't want to leave the painting." I said, "I'll go, you carry on with the painting", and Hugh readily agreed. The only trouble was we were not too sure where the nearest fish and chip shop was. We had been told of one in Albert Road, on a bus route, about mile away, so off I went. I left Hugh up the ladder, painting away, and got to the shop, purchased my fish and chips and went to the return bus stop just outside. I noticed a noisy public house next door and hoped the bus would not be too long in coming.

I had been waiting for ages, when the pub door opened, a sailor came rolling out and making his way to the bus stop, started chatting me up. I have always been afraid of people the worse for drink, and this man was well in his cups and getting friendlier every minute. I never said a word outwardly, but inside I was having quite an argument with God, and asking Him, "Why have you brought me to this place, you know I'm scared and cannot even stand the smell of drink, why don't you do something, you could at least make the bus come." Just then, the bus came round the corner and thankfully I got on. My one idea was to put as much room as possible, between the sailor and myself, and seeing a seat by the door sat down, he had to go lower down the bus. As the conductor came for my fare, the sailor, who was watching me, stood up, and said, "I'll pay for her ticket." Then pointing to me, he said to everyone on the bus, "When I came out of the pub swearing and drunk, I started talking to her, but something has happened to me, I'm sober and I cannot swear, I don't know what it is, but it's all to do with her."

I wanted to hide under the seat and was completely out of my depth. My prayers had not been good and holy, but desperate, because of fear, but God had answered me in a way I could not believe possible. He had sobered the man up and stopped him from swearing. Getting home I found Hugh still up the ladder, but further on with his painting, and only too ready to come down for his fish and chips, and a cup of tea.

That night, we made a covenant with God, telling Him that from now on, we would trust him to keep and protect our children, in any situation, we could not always be with them, but we knew that with Him, they, and we, would always be safe.

Some years later, while at my kitchen sink one morning, I saw a shadow pass the window and wondered what it was. I went out of the kitchen into the corridor leading into the yard and saw a table neatly laid out with motor bike parts. Martin was at the motor bike stage of life, we often had a group of his friends, seriously discussing their motor bike problems, sometimes we had more than one machine in the yard, it was all part of growing up. I saw a man in the corridor, wearing blue overalls, and carrying a toolbox. He looked surprised and guilty when he saw me. "What are you doing here?" I asked. He said, "I've come to mend your washing machine." I knew this was not true. "What make is it?" was my next question. "I don't know," he replied. I looked him straight in the eye, realising he had more than enough motorbike parts at hand, if he wanted to get rough. I felt angry, and with a righteous indignation in me, a new experience, I said to him, without the least bit of fear, "Get out, you are a liar, an absolute liar, get out, and don't forget to close the doors, and the gate behind

50

you." He turned round and went out without a word, closing the back door, the yard door and the side gate after him. While this was happening, Hugh was in the study, it was a big house and I'm not surprised he had not heard a thing. When I told him, he asked, "Why didn't you call out for me?" I said, " I'm sure, if I had taken my eyes off him, he would have hit me with one of the motor bike parts." We just thanked God for His help in such a situation, and probably had a cup of tea!

One of the many problems we faced was a lack of leaders, an elderly lady ran the Women's Fellowship, in the "temporary" church hall, a Nissen hut! Another elderly lady ran a Young Wives' Group in the vicarage, one of their activities was playing bingo, and some of the group were not very young. After a few weeks, I was asked if I would take over the leadership of the Young Wives, but asked for time to think and pray the matter over. We could not allow bingo in our home, and knew that with such a group already in existence, it would not be easy to start another with younger women. The only decision was to close down this group, and ask them to join the Women's Fellowship, or the Mother's Union, leaving the way open for a Young Wives' Group later on, and that would not be easy! I asked the leader to come to the vicarage, but she said, "No, I would rather we met in the Nissen hut."

Going to the hut, on the day we had arranged, I opened the door, and was amazed to see about 20 members, sitting at tables, although I had only arranged to meet the their leader, and as they saw me, the barrage started. Anything they could say about church members or the church was shouted at me. If I closed the meeting down, the church would lose the money they made at a church sale once a year. I hardly had a chance to open my mouth. There was more, but fortunately I have forgotten, I only remember being in the hall about ten minutes and very glad to get outside again. This was a side of church life I had never seen before and was quite shaken; it was obvious they thought I would give in to them. They were about twenty in number, I was only one, and as I could not make half the noise they were

51

making, I let them have their say. I must say here, that some of them came to church, and it was quite a while before I was able to trust them again. Before leaving, I stood up and said, "As from today, this group is not part of the work and witness of St.Luke's, we have a Women's Fellowship and Mother's Union, and I would suggest you join one of these. I am going to start a Young Wives' Group, for mothers with children still at school, you are welcome to come, if you are eligible", and made for the door, relieved to leave the shouting and tension behind me.

I don't think the situation could have been handled any differently. Many stories about the new vicar and his wife were circulating around the parish; we learnt afterwards that people were wondering how we were going to tackle the problems of dancing and bingo, endless jumble sales and raffles. As a former Organising Secretary for the Church Pastoral-Aid Society, Hugh was known to have standards some St.Luke's people must have forgotten. As Christians, we believed God did not need dancing, jumble sales, raffles and bingo to raise money, and were prepared to trust him to meet our needs, as individuals, and as a Church.

One interesting knock-on effect from this incident was brought home to us quite by chance. Hearing the dust-cart along the road, I collected the rubbish from the kitchen bin and went out, just in time to see a dustman coming in the yard door and said to him, "Good, I've just caught you." He laughed and said, "That's all right, but I'm pleased I don't have to deal with bingo cards from your dustbin any more."

The family settled well in school, Martin got his Grammar School place, and in the home we were a normal family. In the parish though, it was a different story, tales got around that were not true and we realised it was up to us to prove ourselves by our lives, and that is always where the going gets tough.

For six months we had the help of a young missionary candidate in the parish. Jane had been advised to get some parochial experience, before going abroad. She loved every minute of the work; in fact Hugh said to me, "Jane works as though she had only six months to live." She had an open top car and one day, just outside our gate, she saw a woman the worse for drink, (this was just after 2 pm when the pubs closed.) and offered her a lift home. She invited Jane into her bedsit. On the table were a newspaper, a loaf of bread, some cheese, and a tin of condensed milk. Feeling a little embarrassed; she asked Jane if she would call and see her when she had tidied up a bit. Jane agreed and went on the suggested day. As she left, she met the owner of the house who told her, "We don't want your sort here, don't ever come to this house again." This hurt Jane, she had so much love for people, and the ones she longed to help would not, or could not, listen. About a week later the parish was buzzing with the news of a bedsit house in Blackfriars Road. The owner had been smoking in bed, then he had fallen asleep and somehow his bedding caught alight and he died. It was the house where Jane had been told she was not wanted. I cannot remember the full details, but these are the facts, and they really shook us.

As her children came to Sunday School, Jane called on Elsie, and found she had just come out of hospital with her eighth child, and now had a back problem that prevented her from bathing the baby. As a trained nurse and midwife Jane was only too happy to help until Elsie was better. She said to me, "It's wonderful to be holding a baby again. When we start a Young Wives Group, I know Elsie will come, she's really interested."

A few months later we started the group in the vicarage and Elsie came along. With eight children she had her hands full, she was always bright and happy, but very tired. Often she would fall asleep in the chair, apologising when she woke up saying, "It's so quiet and peaceful here, I just can't help it." I was pleased that our home had such a relaxing effect on her and she knew we were happy to have her in the group, even if she did nod off at times.

Over the years we got to know Elsie well, she was such an encourager, and had an open, uncomplicated way of talking about her faith. She needed major surgery and was naturally concerned about the family and how they would manage while she was away. We prayed for her, the family, the surgeon who would operate on her, and her well being after surgery. She made such a remarkable recovery; the hospital let her go home early. When she went for a check-up the surgeon said, "We are surprised at your quick recovery" Elsie replied, "I'm not, I go to a church where the people believe in prayer, my friends have been praying for me and for you too." Her uncomplicated faith was a lesson to me, as it must have been to the surgeon, and made me wonder if I would have answered like that.

She was well supported by her husband Ray, who would take care of the children while she was out. The area where Elsie lived was due for demolition, and later the family moved into a large council house on the outskirts of Portsmouth. That did not deter Elsie, she still came to church and the Young Wives' Group, Ray would bring her by car or she would get the bus. We are still in touch, all the children are married and her last letter told me that she and Ray have seventeen grandchildren.

But to get back to Jane, after her time with us, she left to get ready for her work abroad. Her parents lived in the Hampshire village of East Meon and owned the village shop. This meant Jane could pop in and see us. One Sunday she came to lunch and had lots of catching up to do on people. God had given her a great love for ordinary people and an amazing capacity to reach out to them with the love of Jesus. After we had finished talking, she went rather quiet and said, "I've been having bad headaches at times and my eyes are playing up, I'm having tests and probably need glasses. I don't think I should drive home, would you please ring my father and ask if he will come and fetch me." A short time later we were told Jane had a brain tumour, and was going into hospital for treatment, and possible surgery.

With a doctor friend, I went to visit her in a Southampton hospital. Jane did not recognise us, and after a short time we knew we should leave her. Conversation was not possible, but as I left, I touched her hand and said, "God bless you Jane." We were amazed to hear Jane say, "Blessed assurance, Jesus is mine." She did not get the rest of the verse, but we found a piece of paper and wrote down the words of the first verse and chorus, and gave it to the sister in charge of the ward. Explaining she was a doctor, Deidre said, "Jane remembers these words, they could be a comfort to her, if she wakes up, please would you read them to her."

Jane died about two months later, quietly at home. She had just given a short talk showing slides of her time in Africa to a group in the village. Arriving home, she said to her parents, "I'm tired, I'll go and have a rest", and quietly went into the presence of her Lord. Dear Jane, we loved her and missed her, but rejoiced that she was with the Lord she loved and out of pain. As we thought about this, we thanked God that Jane had not left her family and was still in England when the problems started. Had she not spent six months with us at St Luke's she would have been in Africa, away from her family and friends who loved her. We thank God for every remembrance of Jane.

One day off we were busy in the garden when Joan came. She had some problem about Guides and needed Hugh's help. We chatted over the fence as Joan could see we were getting down to an overgrown garden, and she did not want to disturb us more than necessary. When her husband, Bill, came home from work they discussed Guides - and the new vicar and his wife! Joan said, "I thought they were nice people, and maybe, we should give them a bit of support." They started coming to church on the following Sunday, we were delighted and enjoyed getting to know them, they had a daughter and two sons, one at the Grammar school with Martin, but not in his form.

Later Bill and Joan came on to the PCC, and as Christians, were a great encouragement. Financially the church was having a hard time, but Hugh would not allow the methods the previous vicar had used to raise money. We had some difficult meetings, some for us and some against. With few Christians on the PCC, how could we expect otherwise, our prayer was, "O God, bring some born again Christians into the church, and on to the PCC."

With the help of the Church Pastoral-Aid Society we were able to look for a replacement for Jane. Hugh felt a Lady Worker, as they were then called, would be a greater help than a curate, at that time. Pamela, our friend in CPAS work in Bristol, suggested we contacted Patsy Jenks as she was nearing the end of her training at Dalton House Ladies' College. She was a physiotherapist, but had felt a call to parish work. We liked her from the start. At first she seemed quiet, but we soon realised she had a delightful sense of humour and was a great favourite with the children, especially Ruth, I enjoyed having someone to talk to at my own level and we became good friends.

By this time Robert, from Guyana, and Mary, from Southall, both students at Portsmouth Polytechnic were coming to church and to our weekly Bible study in the vicarage. They did us good. Mary had difficulties at her digs, her landlady was holding seances in the house, and being so upset by this, she planned to give up her degree course and go home. The first we knew of this was when she came round to ask if we could keep her trunk in the vicarage, until it could be collected. Hugh was the only one in when Mary called, she said afterwards, "I cried so much on Hugh's shoulder, and made it so wet that he needed to change his shirt." The reason for the tears! Hugh had said to Mary, "You can come and live at the vicarage and finish your degree course, you will always be disappointed if you give up now." And so Mary became just like a member of the family. As an only child, she was thrown in at the deep end, but I know she enjoyed her stay with us, just as much as we enjoyed having her.

A year or two afterwards a young student asked Mary if she would go out with him. Mary liked him and agreed, later she asked us if she could bring him to tea and then to church, we were delighted to say yes. And so John came into our lives. Sometime later, during an Eric Hutchings Crusade, John was led to the Lord by Roger Davies, one of the team members, in Hugh's study. We kept in touch and eventually Hugh married them in Mary's home parish. Ruth was bridesmaid, wearing a beautiful red velvet dress, and Martin and Paul were ushers. Later still, John felt God was saying the ordained ministry was to be his sphere of work, and after training, he turned his collar round and is now a vicar in the Fen country, with a lovely family of two daughters and a son.

Robert was often at the vicarage, he first started coming between lectures to play the piano and have a cup of tea. We must have been one of the few vicarages with live 'music while you work' two mornings a week! He too became one of the family, and still is. The thing I noticed about the family was our security in each other. This enabled us to reach out to others in need and draw them into our family circle, we were not perfect in any way, but we cared about our friends, they knew it, and responded to our love and care. I have always been moved by the simple text "He puts the solitary into families". Again and again, we have proved this to be true.

With Robert's musical input into our family, Paul and Ruth said they would like to play the guitar, they put Christmas and birthday money towards this end and each bought a Spanish guitar. They practised hard, and were surprised at the effect this had on their fingers. Robert suggested white spirit applied to the tops of the fingers would help harden them off, and it worked. One of my precious memories is of Paul and Ruth, singing "The streets of London". .

We had a midweek Bible study and prayer meeting, about eight of us sat round our big dining table. In addition to Hugh, Patsy, Mary, Robert and myself, there were three ladies, all in their eighties. These dear people told us that, during the interregnum, they had prayed every night at 9 pm, "Please God, send the man of your choice to St Luke's." It was humbling to hear that they believed the Lord had answered their prayer when we came to the parish!

However we were experiencing many problems and some opposition to our methods. We had now been at the church for five years and had not seen any real break-through. Feeling discouraged, we began to ask God if we were in the right place.

One morning, after a particularly difficult church council meeting, I could not concentrate on things in the house, and Hugh could not concentrate on things in the study! I made a cup of coffee and took it into the study; as we talked things over, we came to the conclusion that after five years at St Luke's, we had had enough, and it was time to go. It was possible to move the children without too much disruption to their school life, and Hugh thought he might contact CPAS and ask them if they had any openings through their patronage work just then. The postman came; the only mail was a duplicated magazine called, "The Church in Industrial Areas". As he read it, Hugh said to me, "I'm sure God sent this magazine today." He read an article, written by a vicar who had faced the same problems we were facing, and being discouraged, was ready to leave his church, but something made him stay, neither of us can remember what it was. After that, the church was greatly blessed, and he said, "If anyone is in the same position, hold on, I am sure God will yet give His blessing." It seemed as if some churches only came to life through toil and tears, we felt that St.Luke's was such a church.

Hugh felt God was saying, "Stay." I was all for going, I'd had enough. Hugh prayed, and put out a fleece, "If we have one bit of encouragement today, we will stay, if not, we will take it that God wants us to go." It was a Wednesday, nothing happened all day, I was pleased.

The time for the Bible study drew near. At about 7.20 pm, the doorbell rang, Hugh answered it and found Joan and Bill at the front door and automatically took them into the study. I was in the kitchen, and hearing their voices, went into the study to say hello. They were all smiling, as Hugh said, "Bill and Joan have come to the Bible study, they feel that after last night's council meeting, we needed some encouragement!"

My first thoughts were, "I don't want to stay, Lord, I've had enough." But we had put out a fleece and God had given us His clear answer, "I want you at St Luke's." How I thank and praise God that we stayed - for another seven years!

58

In the New International Version John 1v.16 reads: "From the fullness of His grace we have all received one blessing after another." This proved to be our experience, I'm not saying everything was perfect, we still had many problems, but our Heavenly Father was giving us His blessings, one after another, through the people He brought to St.Luke's, starting with Bill and Joan, and we rejoiced in His love.

Over twenty years after we had left St Luke's, we joined Joan and Bill as they celebrated their Golden Wedding, and inevitably we chatted about old times. Bill told us, "On the Wednesday evening Joan and I came to our first Bible study, I was gardening, but someone kept on saying, "Go to the Bible study." Eventually he went in to Joan saying, "I must go to the Bible study tonight", and Joan, bless her, replied, "I'll come with you."

CHAPTER 6
ENCOURAGEMENT AND ANSWERED PRAYER

Hugh came back from a meeting of local evangelical ministers one day with the exciting news that Eric Hutchings and his team were to be invited to conduct a Portsmouth Crusade in the Guildhall, lasting for one month. He felt that this would be both an opportunity and a challenge for us, and set about encouraging our people to support in every way possible.

About this time, the yearly intake for St.Luke's Church School meant that we saw a few more Sunday School children, and some parents coming to Church, to qualify for a place in the school, because of Church connections. As soon as they had a place, such visits usually ceased! If a child was unsuccessful, we often had an irate father on the doorstep demanding to know why the vicar had not given his child a place. The school was originally started by a former vicar of St.Luke's, to provide schooling for local children of all ages, but now it is a diocesan senior school, and every parish is entitled to recommend children for admittance.

Among our morning congregation I noticed a mother and father and two boys, the elder obviously ready to move school at the start of the autumn term. Talking to them, I discovered they lived in the parish, and were keen to get their eldest son, Paul, into St Luke's School. Marjorie and Alan said, "If we want our sons to get a place, we feel it's only right to come to church." After a few weeks I said to Marjorie, "We have a Young Wives' Group, are you interested in coming?" I got a definite "No, I'm too busy with the family". I could understand, and left it like that, for the moment.

When the crusade started, we encouraged all our people to attend. One Sunday evening Marjorie, Alan, Paul and Kevin went along, and to our joy all went up to the front for counselling. Alan was not sure, and rightly, would not do anything about the matter until he was. His counsellor visited his home and they had more than one session together. One night, it all fell into place, and St.John 3 verse 16 became a living reality in Alan's

61

life - this was what he had been searching for. That night, after his friend had left, he went to his tool box, realising he had some tools with a government stamp, and got them ready to take into work the following morning. Working in an office in the Dockyard, Alan had easy access to tools, and it was so easy to borrow something he needed to do a job at home and forget to return it. The people he worked with thought he was mad, they said, "Nobody would ever know, keep them." Alan knew he was not mad, but had just come to his senses.

The change in this family was evident for all to see, and straight faces were replaced by the joy of the Lord, a glow that says, "Jesus lives here." This story was repeated in many lives, God was giving "us one blessing after another." The church was coming alive, young people, school friends, older people too, there was no limit to the work of the Holy Spirit, It was a mini revival. Hugh had the tremendous joy of seeing about thirty people connected with St Luke's come forward in response to the appeal made by Eric Hutchings each evening. We were greatly impressed too by the team members Eric brought with him; people like Russell and Betty Lou Mills and Geoff Perceval on the music side, and Roger Davies and Ken Coventry heavily involved with the organisation of the rallies. Roger stayed in our home for the whole period and became a friend to all the family

I have no idea when Carol first came to St Luke's, a quiet person, it was almost possible to overlook her, but her work with the Guides and Brownies, and in the Sunday school, has stood the test of time. She was always there, quietly supporting and encouraging. We know that the secret behind her consistent and effective service for the Lord was her own personal walk with Him. The church is made up of such people, who without fuss, but gently and with a deep sense of doing God's will, get on with "It", whatever the task is. I know they will get their reward in heaven, because God is not like us, he never overlooks anyone.

Robert along with Paul and Ruth, another Paul, Isobel, and one or two more young people, formed a singing group they called the "Blue Chords". By this time we had quite a number of teenagers coming to church and felt the need for such a group to lead the congregation in the new songs that were being written by Michael Baughen - later Bishop of Chester - and others. The girls in the group wore blue dresses and the boys multi-coloured striped blazers with a blue background, bought at a C. & A. sale for £1 each. They looked attractive, smart and most presentable. Although not in the group, Martin also bought a blazer, at such a give away price, it was silly not to.

We knew there was a need for someone to lead the young people and God brought Alan and Christine Dodds to us. Alan was a Church Army evangelist, Christine a schoolteacher. The local council housing department agreed to rent them accommodation in the parish. Alan was a great personal worker and had an amazing way with young people, a gift from God. Another of Alan's gifts was playing the guitar and leading singing. We soon knew many more of the new songs and had great times of fellowship in the vicarage, after the evening service. Alan was pleased to find a ready made singing group, and was soon using them beyond the parish as well as at our own services - about this time the name was changed, perhaps more in line with the secular groups springing up everywhere in the sixties. It became simply, "Alive"!

A song we will always remember from this period had words written by a friend of Alan's. Alan composed the music:

Be with me Lord every hour of the day in all I do and say;
Let sin pass me by, make me realise that I
Need You every step of the way.
Time hurries by and troubles arise in this world full of sorrow and strife;
But when I walk with You there is nothing to fear
For You are the Lord of my life.
Friends come and go but I'm never alone, for with You I've got everything
You know all my needs and understand these
For You are the Lord of my life.

We still get Paul and Ruth to sing it to us when we get the family together, and think it's a song that deserves to be better known than it is - the tune is really catchy!

Over the years much of the parish was demolished and people were moved into council housing in various areas, some well outside the city. Then rebuilding started and we became, after a year or two, a parish of tower blocks, the whole face of the area was changed.

Martin used his camera well while the work was going on, giving us a photographic history of our very interesting parish. When we first went to St.Luke's most of the houses were terraced dwellings, with small back gardens. Many of them were beautifully kept, and the gardens a joy to behold, but they were so small that in such places, when Hugh took a funeral, the coffin had to go out of the front room window! But other houses were run-down and in need of repair, and people did not seem to bother. Families lived close together, granny down one street, with daughter and family in another, and when the children married, they stayed close to their parents. It was very much a community; granny would sit on a chair outside her door and just watch the world go by, the children would play in the street. They felt very lonely in the high rise flats. The cry was, "We don't see anyone." The view from some flats was amazing, but most people had lived next door to their neighbours for years and missed them.

The family service, held once a month, was growing rapidly, mums, dads, and children all came along. Alan and Marjorie ran the Sunday School. Ruth helped teach and Paul played his guitar. Our children, now in their teens, were in the Youth Club, run by Alan Dodds. All this did not happen overnight, but we were so encouraged to see the way God worked, always bringing people to Himself through the cross of Jesus.

Just to pick out a few of the blessings, through people. Our organist, Kathleen, trained the choirboys and got the shortened name of Katie. Paul was in the choir and I feel sure he had a hand in this. Even to day we talk of Katie and not Miss ... so much nicer.

The young wives, under Katie, formed a choir, but we needed men. With a little persuasion, Alan joined us and we discovered he had a good voice. Robert, with his love of music, was another valuable member of the choir. Others joined us as we started practising for a performance of Stainer's "The Crucifixion", to be held in St Luke's on Good Friday evening with combined church choirs participating.

The great day came, we were excited and nervous, but we knew our parts well, Katie had worked wonders with common clay. The church was full and we sang the wonderful words of that sacred oratorio with praise and thanksgiving in our hearts. Katie was proud of her choir and said, "You did very well, I'm so pleased with you." Praise indeed!

The following Sunday morning, after the service, Joan, who was one of the first "Young Wives", came to me and said, "Grace, I must talk to you." She looked anxious and I asked her, "What's the problem?" I have never forgotten her answer. She said, "I am not a Christian." Joan was a gentle, quiet person, with a delightful sense of fun; she was married with two little girls. I looked at her and said, "How do you know this?" She replied, "While we were singing 'God so loved the world', the words made me realise I did not know Jesus as my Saviour, what can I do about it?" I asked her, "Are you sure about this?" she answered yes. My next question surprised even me. "Joan, if you died tonight, would you go to heaven?" Her answer was as direct as mine: "I know jolly well I wouldn't." With people milling around us, and the girls wanting to get home for lunch, this was obviously not the time for serious talking. We arranged a time, convenient to her, and Patsy, when they could quietly sort things out. Talking this over with Patsy later, she said, "Joan had no assurance and was searching, the words of John 3.16 made it so clear and all she needed was to be led to Jesus as her Saviour." Praise the Lord!

Jim and Mary and their daughter, Barbara, were involved with the church when we first arrived at St Luke's. Barbara was a guide and Jim was always so helpful when manpower was needed. He was so reliable, Hugh valued his friendship greatly, and his expertise, for instance, in the matter of redecorating the church. We have a lasting memory of Jim perched high up on a very long ladder, and with a paintbrush tied to a broom handle, just reaching the apex above the chancel! Like Alan, he needed to think things through. We called on them one evening and found Jim reading his prayer book, he was sorting something out, a remarkable man, with a quiet, gentle faith, based on love and truth. Jim is the only man I have ever known to sit and read the prayer book at home! Barbara married, but never lost her touch with St Luke's. Jim and Mary moved away from the area, but kept their contact with us. Mary helped when there was need, like Jim she was reliable, they were a great family. Sadly, after we left, Jim died suddenly. I always think of him as one of God's gentleman; it was a privilege to know him.

Paul and Ruth were keen to have piano lessons and Katie said she would teach them, but we did not have a piano, or the money to buy one. Coming back from shopping one day I found a lady waiting on the doorstep and asked if I could help. She said "We are being re-housed and will not be able to take the piano, would you have any use for it? We could deliver it on the day we move." Inwardly I said, "Thank you Lord", outwardly I said, "Yes, we would." I explained, we needed a piano, as our children wanted to start lessons, and we would be very happy to accept their kind offer. After a time Paul decided to stop lessons, but Ruth kept on with them.

Martin, Paul and Ruth in turn all passed their eleven plus and went to local Grammar Schools. Our family were growing up, but were all at different schools, homework became the order of the day. We were fortunate, with such a large house, and separate bedrooms, they were able to study quietly on their own. At this stage, we started collecting desks, I don't remember where they all came from, but each had a desk in their bedroom. The wonderful way God supplied our needs was past finding out, curtains, carpets, £200 for driving lessons, pianos, desks, what to say in difficult situations, the children's schools, the supply was as endless as our needs, and our needs were always met.

Around this time Paul saw a guitar in a second-hand shop for £25 and was very keen to buy it, but it was a lot of money in those days, especially when your parents were not in a position to give you a cheque for that amount! We suggested he might get a job of some kind and save up for it, as long as his homework did not suffer. As Paul's school was quite a way from home, he went by bus. By the bus stop was a music shop, going in one day he looked around, and picking up a guitar noticed it was out of tune, and mentioned this to the proprietor who said, "I cannot tune guitars." Paul answered, "I can, would you like me to tune it for you?" As Paul put it down, he was asked, "Would you like to come in after school and work in the shop, I will pay you so much a week. Paul was thrilled; he had got a job himself and came home really pleased with himself. We were so pleased as this meant he could start saving.

All went well until one afternoon a young man came into the shop with a guitar and case. He asked the owner, "How much will you give me for this?" An amount was mentioned, but the young man exclaimed, "It's worth much more than that, and I need the money." "That is all I can give you." was the reply, and rather foolishly he accepted the offer. Paul heard all this and knew his boss had taken an unfair advantage of the young man. Once he left the shop Paul was asked to write out a price tag, for a greatly increased sum, and put it in the window. He answered, "No, I cannot do a thing like that and will not work for you any more." The next morning waiting for the bus, Paul saw the guitar in the window, with a price tag he would not lower himself to write!

Paul was home earlier than usual that night and told me his story. I agreed that he had done the right thing, but we both knew it had put the cherished dream of a really good guitar a long way from his price range.

The next Sunday Hugh's sister Pen, and his father, came over from Bognor for tea and then came to the evening service with us. I noticed Pen having quite a conversation with Paul and saw her give him a slim booklet. His face was one big smile as he came up and said, "Auntie Pen has been putting £1 into this Post Office Savings book every birthday since I was born, and it's just enough for me to buy the guitar now!"

We were thrilled that God had acted in such a way. Pen, who was Paul's godmother, told us later, "I knew Paul could make use of the money, it was better than just leaving it in the Post Office."

When we first arrived at St Luke's I had a strong feeling we should get a dog, and started looking in the local papers, and got books from the library on dogs. It had to be a dog that was good with people, and with such a big house, we felt it should be a big dog, but above all, it had to be a dog the children would love and know as their friend. A tall order! For sometime, no dog came up to our expectations. I had a birthday and kept all my gifts of money towards buying "the dog". It was eight pounds in all, not much, but God said, "The cattle on a thousand hills are mine", and for the sake of the family, I decided to include dogs in that promise as well.

The Rural Dean and his wife invited us to lunch, and sitting in their lounge, we knew our search was over when two golden retrievers walked in and made friends with us. It was love at first sight; they were beautiful and met all our requirements. We knew such dogs would be expensive and we only had eight pounds, but we had proved again and again "With God all things are possible", so we trusted God and waited.

We did not get a local paper regularly, but one evening I found one on the lounge table, and automatically picked it up to look at the "Dogs" advert and read "Golden Retriever puppies for sale, ready in four weeks, eight guineas."

That is how Dexter came into our lives. Always with a pet, one asks, what shall we call it? Our puppy was one you could not ignore, he had an impish, loveable, friendly personality, and in fact he was everybody's friend. We had many discussions, but could not hit on the right name. Hugh and the boys were (and still are) cricket fans. Ted Dexter was doing very well for Sussex at this time and while talking about Dexter and his success Hugh suddenly said, "How about calling him Dexter?" We all agreed, and so Dexter he became.

He was my shadow during the day, but gave the children his full attention after school. When I went to the front door he would follow me, giving his friendly welcome to all that called. But there was one exception to this. When we had tramps at the front door, he would bark, even before I opened the door, and stand in front of me, his hackles up, ready to protect me. How he knew I did not know. He certainly kept undesirable callers away. Someone was just turning into the vicarage drive and overheard two men talking, they said, "We won't go there, they have a big dog." He never barked at "Charlie" or regular callers, but those just passing through would often walk away when they heard Dexter bark.

I could fill a book with Dexter stories; he certainly came up to all our expectations. Obviously feeding such a big dog could have been expensive, but our butcher kept all his pieces for me, at one shilling a time, and with biscuits and, of all things, grated carrots, he was well fed.

Dexter was accepted by all our family and friends. He loved a St.Luke's bank holiday ramble, and would go from group to group when the sandwiches came out to see what he could scrounge. Family holidays too were his great delight; he had us all together then.

A few years ago, at different times, Martin, Paul and Ruth visited us in our retirement, and said "Dexter made so much difference to our lives at Portsmouth." God is interested in every aspect of our lives, even to choosing a dog suitable for a vicarage family.

All through this book, so far, I have implied we were hard pressed financially. That was so true, and many of our clergy friends were in the same position. Every penny had to count, but our very need threw us back on God. Talking to a parishioner, she told me how difficult they were finding things financially. She was thinking of going back to work, they could not live on her husband's money, and mentioned what he was paid. It was more than the stipend Hugh received. We had the house, but heating was always a big problem, and the size of the house meant that the vicar's wife needed help and not all churches paid expenses. I am so thankful things have changed, they needed to, but one precious lesson I learnt was that you could trust God, even with your back against the wall and no way out. He meets all our needs. I can only add to that "Praise the Lord, Amen."

Grace, Hugh and Dexter on the South Downs 1974

CHAPTER 8
HOUSEBOAT AND HOUSEPARTY

Talking over the progress of the book, this far, Hugh said, "You have not mentioned Sue or the boat." My difficulty is what to leave out. Obviously, some things are best left unsaid, but again, Hugh is right, the boat is very much family, Sue is the church at prayer.

We found holidays a necessity, it was important to get away. We camped and had holiday cottages, but even in those days, the price was getting far beyond our reach. Easter was late one year, and because of this, we decided to enquire about a houseboat holiday on Hayling Island. We had an old car, and made the trip round to the Kench on the island. We knew the area fairly well, and sometimes went across the ferry from Portsmouth, an interesting journey, and quite reasonable, as far as cost was concerned. Sometimes, the boats had a "To let" notice with the telephone number of the owner, if people were interested.

On this occasion we saw quite a few boats, but no "To let" notices. A man passed by on a bike, he looked like a local and we asked him if there were any houseboats to let. He said, "No, but there is one for sale, and I have the key. Would you like to look over it?" Never having been on a houseboat before, we were all keen to look around, but Hugh was hesitant, he said quietly to me, "We cannot buy a houseboat." I knew that, but wanted to see over it all the same! Dexter was with us and was getting as excited as we were.

When we first saw the boat, we all thought it looked like Noah's ark. It had a big galley with a full size Calor gas stove, a good sink and draining boards; plenty of cupboards, cooking utensils, saucepans, cutlery, and china. In the saloon was a table and two red leather settees, a settee bed, and cord carpeting on the floor. Through a door into a corridor were two bedrooms, one with a bunk bed, one with a single bed, an Elsan toilet and a hatch to get up on the roof. Obviously just right for five people, and a dog!

The man was keen to sell. We thought, "If only we had the money." Wisely the man gave us the telephone number of the owners and we said goodbye. Looking back at the boat, we knew it would be a wonderful place for holidays and days off. At high tide, it floated, but was kept secure by strong chains. With blue check curtains, black pitch up to a high beam all round the boat and white paint above the beam, it was the perfect answer to our holiday problem.

As it was our day off, we went on to Bognor and told Hugh's parents about the boat. The children were so excited, but we made them realise we had only looked over it and could not possibly buy it. We had a meal with the family and left for home. Later that evening we had a phone call from Hugh's parents. They were willing to lend us the money; we could pay back so much a month. Of course we said, "Yes please!" We started this scheme, but after a time they said, "The boat is yours." When their family were small Mum and Dad had faced the same problem, they knew our need to get away from the vicarage at times, and knew we would enjoy the boat to the full. We certainly did! We had wonderfully relaxed holidays, and soon made friends with the other boat owners and their children.

For Dexter, the boat was all he could ask for, His greatest delight was to lie on the gangplank and wait until high tide brought the water up to his tummy, and only then would he move. I was sitting on the gangplank with Dexter one-day when a couple passed by. They asked, "Is he your dog? Every morning he comes up to The Point, swims round in a half circle, dries himself on the stones and sand, has a good shake, and then goes away, just like an old man having his early morning swim."

We were able to offer the boat to friends, who, like us, found holidays too expensive for a family. There was dear Fred, once a sailor in the Royal Navy and a grand Christian worker, a real evangelist. He and his family had a couple of holidays on the boat. Brother John and his wife, Pat, and their children loved going there for a break. Friends he made at the Kench gave him a rowing boat. We were given a canoe; people were so friendly and were always ready to help each other. We all have wonderful memories of our houseboat holidays.

With our staff of Hugh, Alan and Patsy and some interested church members, we began thinking about a Church houseparty. Hugh's love of Eastbourne made it our first choice and with the help of a friend he made enquiries about the student hostel of the School of Domestic Economy. They could take us and the price was most reasonable, in fact, on our information sheet we were able to write, "Nearer to the sea than the Grand Hotel!" If I remember correctly, every bedroom but one looked out over the sea, which was just across the road, an ideal spot. We self-catered and bulk bought from a Cash and Carry. A friend of Patsy's from college was willing to do the cooking, with help. We had a rota for washing up and laying the tables. Hugh and Alan planned the evening talks. One I remember was "Bed and breakfast for 2 ½ new pence", or "Bed and breakfast with Simon the tanner". (A dreadful pun, concerning the story of Peter lodging by the sea at the house of Simon the tanner - this was near the time we were preparing to go decimal!) Someone would be asked to take the morning reading from "Daily Light", before we left the breakfast table, and the rest of the day would be free, unless we planned a day out somewhere. With Alan and his guitar, we were assured of good music, and happy, relaxed worship. Apart from the weather, we were all set for a perfect holiday.

One afternoon I answered the door to a Miss Livingstone. She had heard about the houseparty and wondered if we had room for her, and the family of three adults and two children, with whom she lived. We were only too pleased to say yes. And that is how Sue came into our lives. Sue was a nurse who had been off sick with a bad back for some time, and needed a holiday.

Just how bad the back was we did not realise at first. Sue was on crutches and in a lot of pain. We soon got to know her, as with her family, she started coming to church. She told us God was calling her to be a missionary in Nepal. We knew if

75

this was so, something would have to be done about her back, and her legs and ankles, which were very swollen, but she was always so ready to join in with whatever was going on. The only time she had relief from the pain was in the water, so a group of us went with her to the local swimming baths, where Sue swam like a fish, not using her legs, only her arms.

We arrived for our houseparty at Eastbourne on a bright sunny day, and had perfect weather all the week. Some joined in "Keep fit" around the bandstand, others went for an early morning bathe, and we had outings and rambles and went to St Mary's, Hailsham, for a morning service. One of the churchwardens there was Alan, who had been some three years senior to Hugh at school in the thirties. He and his wife Betty joined us for a barbecue on the beach one evening, Alan bringing a good supply of wood for the fire. This lovely Christian couple were fully involved in the life of both church and town in Hailsham. Alan is still very active in many areas of community life. We also supported and enjoyed the open air services held on Eastbourne sea front. Looking back, I realise what a great responsibility we had, but the fun and togetherness we enjoyed made it all utterly worthwhile. One elderly widow, affectionately known as Mrs P, said to me, "This is the first holiday I've ever had." She was 74 at the time.

Martin and I were walking along the lower promenade one afternoon, it was a beautiful day, the beach was crowded, the tide going out, we were just chatting and enjoying each other's company. Suddenly, Martin said, "Take these, Mum, there is a girl on a Lilo being swept out to sea near the rocks. You stay here." As he said this he took off his watch, and emptied his pockets into my hands, jumped down onto the beach and ran. No one else noticed what was happening, as I have said, the beach was crowded. He reached the girl - the Lilo was not important - and swam with her towards one of the groynes. A man was standing with his arms outstretched towards the girl. As she came out of the water, he took her in his arms, wet as she was, and hugged and kissed her, and then wrapped her in a towel.

While all this was going on my mind was working overtime. Martin was a very good swimmer, he had swum the Southsea annual pier to pier race, and as a trained lifeguard, did duty on Portsmouth beach, so he knew what he was doing. Even so, I was his mother and was anxious for his safety, especially as I thought of the rocks and it was obvious, as I looked out to sea, the girl was very frightened. I could understand how the man felt.

As he handed the girl back to her father Martin said, "Take her home." The father replied, "We are on holiday and staying in a hotel, please come and see me later and we will have a drink, I don't know how to thank you! "

We made straight back to the house and as we walked along, I have a memory of Martin looking down and saying, "I've ruined my trousers!"

I was using the Living Bible for my daily reading at that time it was being published in separate books and Psalms had just come out. The day in question, I had just read Psalm 103, a favourite of mine and verse 3 stuck in my mind, "He forgives all my sins. He heals me." So simple, but so profound.

For some reason I was around the house after lunch and saw Sue and the family come in. She was walking very slowly, and looked in great pain, they had all been round the shops, and Sue had overdone it. I looked at her and said, "You are going to have a couple of hours on the bed", and walked towards her bedroom; she followed me without a word. I helped her into bed, got some water for her to take pain-killing tablets, and she snuggled down. As I looked at her, Psalm 103 verse 3 came into my mind: "He heals me." Before I realised what I was doing, I reached out, put my hand on her head and said, "Lord Jesus, heal Sue."

As I took my hand away, I was overwhelmed by what I had said. Leaving her without a word, I hurried to find Hugh, only to be told he was out. Seeing Patsy, I asked her to come up to our bedroom, and explained what had happened. We read Psalm 103 and knelt down by the bed and prayed for Sue's healing again. Patsy and I had drawn very close to each other, and after our time of prayer and fellowship, I felt much encouraged about the situation.

Sue slept right through the evening meal and put in an appearance, still on her crutches, just before we left the dining room. Patsy and I looked at each other; God had not healed her.

Soon after the holiday Sue was booked to go into hospital again. Looking back now, I know God needed to get us in a position of love, and praise, free from fear and trusting Him with every part of our being as we prayed for Sue. Our Bible reading became deeper, our prayers too. Many from the holiday party knew her needs and we encouraged them and others to pray for Sue daily. This was the church in earnest prayer for a fellow Christian with a great need. Some of us agreed to pray every night at 9 pm. August and September passed. Sue was still in hospital.

Alone in the vicarage one evening, I felt a desperate urge to pray for Sue and went upstairs to our bedroom. I knew God was going to heal her, but how? While praying, the book of Acts came into my mind. Opening my Bible, I knelt down and prayed, "God, I'm not getting up until you show me through your word, how you are going to heal Sue." I read chapter one, chapter two and began chapter three. There in verse 6 was my answer, "I command you in the name of Jesus Christ of Nazareth, walk!"

Patsy came in, she had been driving along, and like me, could not get Sue out of her mind. She had been thinking of the story of the men who let their paralysed friend down through the roof to the feet of Jesus. Jesus healed him. We longed for Him to heal Sue. We knew a visit was necessary and planned to go the next day.

Being new to all this, we felt we should fast and pray, before leaving for the hospital. Hugh and Alan promised to pray. We did not know what we would say, but trusted God to show us each step to take. Not much was said in the car, both of us feeling nervous. Arriving at the hospital, we found Miss

Livingstone, now affectionately known to everyone as "Auntie" with Sue, who was dressed and resting on the bed. My first thoughts were, "Good, today is not the day", but after we had been there a few minutes Auntie said, "I'll go now, I only came to collect any washing, and bring clean clothes", and she left us.

It was a perfect day, the hospital had pleasant grounds, and patients were allowed to go outside and find one of the many chairs, if they wished to rest. We asked Sue if she would like some fresh air and she said she would. So, getting the necessary permission, we went outside.

Sue managed well, but we noticed her ankles and feet were very swollen, and even with crutches, it was hard going for her. Finding a garden seat we sat down and told her why we had come. Sue said, "This morning, I read the story of the men who let down their friend at the feet of Jesus and I prayed, 'Lord, if only I had friends like that." We said, "Sue you have, that's why we are here." Patsy continued, "Sue, while I was driving along last night, I could not get you out of mind, and that story of the man let down to the feet of Jesus by his friends came to my mind too." I said, "I know the Holy Spirit brought Acts Chapter 3 verse 6 to my mind, and as I read 'In the name of Jesus of Nazareth, walk', I knew it was for you."

I went over to a tree, turned round and said, "Sue, in the name of Jesus of Nazareth, walk." Sue said, "I can't." Patsy and I said, "In the name of Jesus you can, just walk." She took a first step, without the crutches and then hesitated. We said, "Peter took the man by the right hand, we will do that if you wish, but there is no need." And in the name of Jesus alone, Sue walked. We were so full of praise and thanksgiving as she reached us by the tree, by this time walking normally.

I cannot emphasise enough that never, under any conditions, should one do such a thing without God's leading. We had been in an agony of prayer and searched our Bibles daily for God's answer; because of this, when God did speak to us, we trusted Him, and did what He told us.

We walked back into the ward, Sue carrying her crutches. Getting back to her bed she said, "This floor is so cold", and looking down at her feet, we saw they were not swollen, just the normal size, we did not know when this happened, but it was further proof that God had healed her.

The next day Hugh took a telephone call from a jubilant Sue saying, "The doctor has just seen me, I can go home whenever anyone is free to collect me."

Sue has been a missionary in Nepal some years now, and has done a wonderful work for God. To us she is almost another Amy Carmichael.

Patsy had been with us over eight years, and felt God was saying she should move on. She went to Liverpool and was much used in her ministry there, as she was later in Camborne, Cornwall, and also in two parishes in inner London. In the last of these appointments, to our surprise, in view of her earlier opinions, but to our pleasure also, she became fully ordained and her vicar was another colleague of ours, from our next parish in Worthing, Neil Jackson.

In the spring of 1995 we had a telephone call from Rosemary, Neil's wife, telling us that Patsy had died. She had had what was thought to be flu, but did not respond to treatment, pneumonia developed and she was taken into hospital, and went into the presence of her Lord a week later. We were shattered; she was always so strong and well. It was not until we had attended a wonderful Thanksgiving Service, in her church at Kensal Rise, London, that we felt at peace. Ruth came with us, and Carol made the journey from Portsmouth; we were so pleased. Our dear Patsy was a special person to all of us.

Rosemary also told us Neil had recently been diagnosed as having lung cancer. He had never smoked in his life and had just started a course of chemotherapy, but he was able to take Patsy's Thanksgiving Service. It was good to see Neil and Rosemary and their family, but with Neil's illness, we knew that a difficult time was ahead and Patsy would be greatly missed. At times like this I cannot understand how people get through without prayer. I certainly could not!

In March 1996, we had a letter from Rosemary telling us that Neil died of lung cancer a few days before. We felt so much for Rosemary, Claire and Philip, our hearts went out to them. We were sad and heavy as we grieved for a dear colleague and friend - a true man of God and Christian gentleman. Neil has heard those words, "Well done, good and faithful servant, enter into the joy of your Lord." As with Patsy, the loss, the grief, the sadness, were all there at such a time. But it's such a comfort to know that Jesus wept, and we can weep also.

When I had finished reading Rosemary's letter, I looked at Hugh and said, "But I'm still here." In January 1993, I had been diagnosed as having an inoperable tumour of my left lung. Neil was the sixth person I knew, or, as in the case of Roy Castle, read about, who had died of this awful disease.

"Jesus wept." The shortest text in the Bible, but how I thank God that His son, "The Lord Jesus Christ", was perfect God and perfect man. And He wept.

I have diverged a bit from Portsmouth, but it was necessary.

Hugh felt our need at this time was a curate for St Luke's. Philip Allen had been with us for some weeks, to get experience in a parish before ordination. We all liked him, he fitted in so well with St Luke's set-up, it was unanimously decided to ask him if he would like to be Hugh's curate, and he said yes. To our delight the Bishop approved and in due course Philip joined us. We were unsuccessful in finding a flat for a single man, and so, after prayerful consideration, it was decided that he should live-in at the vicarage. Some of his college friends were horrified - it was never done! But in this case under God's guiding hand it worked very well indeed and we had a couple of really happy years together. Philip is now well settled in his own parish on the Isle of Wight.

The church was growing, a time of consolidation, we were working so well together, and the youth work was flourishing. Alan and Chris had their first baby, Sarah, but after being with us a few years, they felt it was time to move on, and we knew, like Patsy, they would be missed. This is one of the problems of parish life; people always have to leave! Alan too is now ordained and serving in a parish in Kent.

By now we had been at St Luke's for twelve years. Coming back from shopping one day, just walking along with my pusher, I had a strong feeling we would be moving soon. This was so unexpected; I did not know what to do with such a thought. Without saying anything to Hugh I asked God to take it away, but it would not go. I do not believe wives of clergy should normally be the first ones to think about a move! Of course, once a move is being considered, the family (only) talk about the matter, but it is not discussed with parishioners. At least, that was the procedure at that time.

Three months later, while we were driving back into Portsmouth and being greeted by our high rise blocks of flats, Hugh suddenly said, "I feel it's time to leave St Luke's." I asked how long he had felt this and he answered, "About three months, but I know you are so happy here, we must be absolutely sure it's right." I told him of my feelings three months earlier.

The thought of leaving our dear people was hard indeed, but we both knew that this was the right time to make a move.

CHAPTER 9
PINK PAVEMENTS AND CANCER!

Our next move was to Holy Trinity with St Matthew's, Worthing, in 1975, just along the coast. No eighteen or twenty-one storey blocks of flats filled the skyline, some of the pavements were a delightful shade of pink, with bricks laid on their side making an attractive path, something I appreciated. My mother-in-law rang to ask how we were settling in and was amused when I told her how much I enjoyed the pink pavements. This was an entirely different parish, but we were ready for a change, after twelve years in the heart of Portsmouth, and as we knew by this time, each parish has its own characteristics. We were thrilled to meet many mature Christians, people who had loved and served the Lord for many years.

Eric and Janet ran a thriving youth group in their home and had to take the lounge door off its hinges every Saturday night to get all the young people in! They were ably helped by their 'growing up' family. Eric was churchwarden at Holy Trinity, absolutely dependable, and always knew all that was going on. Janet was very hospitable and a really good cook. She must have made hundreds of cakes for the Missionary Sale. I was amazed at her output! A quiet, gentle person, but with a great sense of fun, at one with us in our thoughts on missionary work, and along with many of the people in both churches, they were great prayer warriors.

Tony was churchwarden at St Matthew's, he was very helpful before we moved into the parish. Working locally, he was able to meet us if we went over from Portsmouth. If his cream/white minibus was outside the vicarage, we knew Tony would be waiting for us inside, as a solicitor he helped us both in many ways and we were grateful. I remember Hugh saying, "I'm looking forward to working with Tony, he has a quiet, clear way of looking at things."

Gwen ran a Bible study in her home and, with Aunt Lou, was a tremendous help to many in the parish. As a clergyman's widow, Gwen knew the need for visiting and keeping in touch when people were ill, especially those in the many nursing homes. She is a small, slim lady with amazing energy and a big smile. Now in her 90th year, she is still the same and still driving her car. Her prayer life was open to God; she seemed to pray about everything and everyone, a real Mother in Israel to many.

The choir, under Brenda, was well supported, some members having served in the choir over fifty years. She worked very well with Hugh, I always think of her as a quiet encourager, and a perfectionist.

One evening Martin came home from the youth club and told me about Simon, his mother was very ill, and he thought she would appreciate a visit. I went along one afternoon and met Belle and her husband, Leslie. It was obvious that she was very ill and very brave, my heart went out to her and the family. The last time I saw Belle was in hospital, I believe Hugh, Leslie and myself had communion with her, and not long afterwards she went to be with her Lord. We grieved with Leslie and Simon, but we could truly thank God that their dear one was with the Lord and out of pain. Again and again we realise the need to get alongside ill and bereaved families, and show that we love them and care, making sure they knew we would always be there if they needed us, but without interfering, and getting in the way. We still have contact with Leslie who continues to have a very caring and practical concern for others in need.

Ruth was teaching in the Sunday School and told us about one of the children, whose mother was in hospital, she had breast cancer and was just getting over surgery. We visited her and I remember thinking, "I would not like to go through this", little realising I was to be in the same position before very long. She died a year or so later, her daughter was nine or ten. No one has the answer to these deep heartaches; indeed there is no answer, apart from Jesus, who fully understands our grief and pain.

Many of the congregation at both churches were elderly ladies who prayed for us, I was reminded of our time at

Felixstowe, and the many who prayed for us while we were there. They could surprise us when talking about the past. One lady, in her eighties, in a nursing home, had been born in China of missionary parents and survived the Boxer Uprising. At one time, Ruth asked me to describe someone we were discussing. I thought a bit and said, "She is elderly, not very tall, has grey hair and wears glasses." Ruth laughed and said, "Mum, you have just described more than half the ladies in the parish!"

St Matthew's had a good "Young Wives Group", most of them worshipped in church with their families, their children were in Sunday School. Holy Trinity had a "Wives Group" for older ladies. We were reaping where someone else had sown; I think we both needed that aspect of the ministry.

Perhaps with two churches, it is not surprising that we met some unusual characters.

My first Sunday evening at Holy Trinity, I was standing at the back of the church after the evening service, chatting to some of the congregation, and was introduced to Miss Knocker, a small lady, but very strong minded, as I later discovered. Addressing her as Miss Knocker, I was told in a sergeant major voice, "Don't call me Miss Knocker, call me Knocker, everyone else does." I was not sure about this, but she said, "I want you to, I like it." And so Knocker she became to Hugh and myself, as she was to everybody else who knew her! Prayer was her lifeline, she had a child-like faith that was unshakeable and she loved Jesus. Her great love was missionary work and for many years she had a missionary prayer meeting in her home. As she grew older she became forgetful, and not so sure of herself. The congregation gathered round her with support, when there was a need. I realised this was a caring congregation and saw more than one instance of Christian love in action. Surely, this is what it is all about.

Another character was Miss Pardoe; she had a great passion for music. One winter, in spite of a heavy cough, she was determined not to miss a concert, and went armed with a bottle of cough mixture in a paper bag and a spoon. Having a front seat in the gallery, she was able to put her cough mixture, in the paper bag, with the spoon alongside, on the balustrade. During the interval she had a dose of cough mixture, but took a long time getting the bottle back into the paper bag, and made quite a noise. The conductor, who knew her, turned, looked up at her and said, "We are ready when you are, Miss Pardoe", and when she said she was ready, he gave a little bow in her direction, turned round and continued with the second half of the concert!

One person I must mention is Gladys. Even as my memories come flooding back, my mind conjures up a delightful, charming lady, always smiling. Never once did I hear her complain, but her story is remarkable. Driving home with her husband, I think from holiday, they stopped, had a meal and continued their journey. Gladys dropped off to sleep and woke up in hospital to be told she had undergone extensive surgery on her face. Later, when she was well enough take it, she was told her husband had died at the wheel of the car. They did not have children, but caring relatives looked after her when she left hospital, some months later. Going back for a check- up, the surgeon did not recognise her at first, he had made such a good job of her face, but her faith and lovely character had done the rest.

Winifred Humby, a former Church Army Sister, had retired to Worthing and lived in a ground floor flat. She had worked with Wilson Carlisle, and his sister, Marie. I enjoyed hearing her talk about the early days of Church Army. She had some wonderful tales to tell, and because of this, I asked if she would come and speak to the Young Wives' Group, she was so young in heart and loved by all who knew her. She answered, "Yes, I would be pleased to come." I suggested she said anything that came into her mind about the early days of Church Army, knowing she had a host of stories to tell about her work, and not bother with notes. One story she told is still clear in my mind, even today. Visiting some blocks of flats, I believe in London, she had to knock on the door, and simply allow the Holy Spirit to guide her from there. Having no knowledge of the occupants this was very good training, as she had to rely on

God if any difficulties arose. One lady opened the door, looking very upset, she had been crying and Winifred asked, "Can I help you?" The mother said, "Come in" and told her, "My son was playing with some friends and got a bad knock in the eye with a ball, we have just got back from hospital, they think he will lose the sight of his eye." Winifred did the one thing she knew would help, and asked, "Can I pray with you?" and the mother readily agreed. When she left, Winifred said, "I'll come back later to see how he is." Her next visit was so different. The boy had been back to hospital, and seen the same doctor, who said, "I don't quite know what has happened, but I'm pleased to say your eye is normal. There is nothing wrong with it, you will not lose you sight."

Although Winifred did not have children of her own, she did have a nephew who loved and cared for his aunt, I don't think we met before her funeral, but he was always in the background, and Winifred was very fond of him. Hugh and I really enjoyed her funeral, it was so triumphant. Many friends and a large contingent of Church Army folk attended the service at Holy Trinity, followed by interment at the cemetery. At the graveside we sang the old chorus, "He lives! He lives! Christ Jesus lives today!" - it was Easter time - and at the close, as we each remembered Winifred in our own way, someone said, "Let's sing the 'Doxology', Winifred was always so full of praise." Someone pitched the note and we really let rip, singing it through twice. The undertakers were surprised, but it was spontaneous and so full of meaning, a tremendous tribute to a lively, happy, well over eighty year old child of God who had gone home to be with Him, and one for whom we could truly thank and praise Him.

By this time Martin was a photographer and enjoying his work. Paul was on an electronics course at Salford University and Ruth was reading history at Reading. They were all growing up and becoming our friends as well as our children.

With two churches to run, Hugh was busy, but happy. One problem was the number of Nursing Homes in the parish, especially as this entailed many sick communions. Our predecessor had had two curates, as he was also chaplain at Worthing Hospital, but we were without any ordained help, as both curates had moved on. One had been curate-in-charge of St Matthew's, but when Hugh made the necessary enquiries for a curate he was told that because of the shortage of clergy he could have one curate, for a limited period only. The "quota" for a parish of our size would in future be one clergyman, even though we had two churches.

I think it was at this time that the Church Council suggested that Hugh had help in the study. Shirley had worked in a bank, but because of her mother's ill health had resigned and was willing to work as Hugh's secretary some mornings. Unless one lives in a vicarage, it is impossible to know how much paper work comes through the letterbox, and I imagine it is worse now! Shirley was a great help, and things in the study became well ordered and up-to-date. We enjoyed getting to know her husband Keith, a keen gardener, and her mother, a grand old lady.

After a few months Neil Jackson, with his wife Rosemary and their children, Claire and Phillip moved into the curate's house just along the road. They soon fitted in and Neil had much to contribute to the life of both churches. We greatly enjoyed our all too brief time of fellowship with them, but it was not long before a call to the North came Neil's way, and he accepted a living in industrial Yorkshire. Their going left a big gap.

As no curate would now be allocated to our parish we were thankful to hear that provision could be made for a Church Army Captain to join us. Hugh already valued the help given by retired clergy living in the area, but now he became absolutely dependent on them, especially for the nursing home ministry. Hugh estimated he took about one hundred sick communions every month in many different nursing and rest homes.

Now the whole area has been reorganised as a Team Ministry, four churches in all, and known as the parish of "Christ the King". The Worthing churches have seen many changes, and with manpower in short supply, a solution had to be found, but these things are never easy for all concerned.

The Church Council agreed that a Church Army officer should be appointed and David Ruddick, with his wife Pat and son Andrew, moved into the curate's house. David had a quiet, but very effective ministry over the next three years or so. With his love for people went a love for nature and the environment. He revelled in the large garden, now his delight, and their new home. This family was much missed when they moved on, in due course, to new work in the West Country.

Quite near the vicarage was a Church School where the Vicar of Holy Trinity, and a neighbouring incumbent, alternated as chairman of the school managers. A young student had been on teaching practice at the school for a term and made a good impression on the staff, especially the Headmaster. The managers met to interview candidates for a teaching post and as Hugh left home he said, "I'm sure the student who has done her teaching practice in the school will get the position, the Headmaster is very keen to have her." On his return he confirmed this fact, but added, "I was very impressed with another of the candidates, a young girl named Alison, in my opinion, she was just as good, and like the other girl is a committed Christian, but unlike her she is an Anglican!" We thought no more about it.

Our Youth Club met with the young people from Broadwater Church in a neighbouring parish. Martin became interested in one of the girls there and eventually brought her home. To our delight it was Alison! She had got another teaching post locally and lived in a flat not far from our vicarage. I was impressed with Alison too, and we were delighted when an engagement was announced and later, when a lovely wedding took place at her home parish in Blackheath. Alison's wedding dress was made of pure silk, not white, but a gentle ivory/ cream, very full and hung in graceful folds around her. She looked beautiful. And nearly twenty years later, we are still impressed with Alison! Reading the above, Hugh said, "She still looks beautiful." I agree!

Ruth completed her degree and was now living at home. By this time Paul was working in Germany, very much involved with computers. Ruth and I went to Holy Trinity one summer evening, and Hugh preached on Revelation 4 verse 1: "A door standing open in heaven". Noticing a young man behind us, we introduced ourselves. Chatting to him at the back of the church later, Ruth asked if he was interested in coming to the young people's meeting, called "Open House", and held in the home of David and Janet, stalwarts of the St Matthew's congregation - he was, and Ruth took him along. And that is how Mark came into our lives!

He told us later that he wanted to go to church that evening and only knew of St Paul's, not very far from Holy Trinity. Getting there at 6.15, he found the doors closed - the service had started at 6 pm! As he walked along, he saw some young people going into a church. The door was open, and he followed them in. He sat behind a lady and her daughter, and had a strange feeling they were to play an important part in his life. The Vicar preached "A door standing open" and his daughter invited him to "Open House". David and Janet opened their home every Sunday night to our young people, and that entailed commitment from all the family. Ruth and Mark became engaged and were later married at Holy Trinity. Ruth insisted that her father should give her away, so Hugh asked one of his retired colleagues, Wilfred Crittle, to perform the ceremony. A very happy choice. As a child in Sunday School I had prayed for Wilfred and his wife who were missionaries in Burma! Our young couple were soon well settled in a little house just outside the parish. At the time, we thought we were very fortunate, having two of our children living so close.

Our congregation were very interested in Ruth's wedding. Two University friends, both named Liz, from Reading, along with Bettina, the daughter of one of the young wives, were bridesmaids. Mark grew a patch of pink/light brown alstroemeria flowers, and bought white daisies, with their lovely yellow centres and greenery, they looked delightful in the baskets which Ruth preferred to bouquets. The bridesmaids' dresses picked up this colour scheme. Ruth carried a basket of white flowers, and with the white, yellow, and pink/light brown alstroemeria baskets, carried by the bridesmaids, it was a very pretty wedding. Jeff drove Ruth and Hugh to church, he was an undertaker, a grand Christian, Hugh knew him quite well. In case that seems odd, Jeff's firm had acquired a new limousine, and Ruth was the first bride to use it!

One of the young people from St Matthew's, Linda, had seen some wedding dresses for sale in Chichester. The shop was selling off all their bridal wear. We went over on a snowy, grey day and Ruth got a beautiful dress for £20, a real bargain. She tried it on in the shop and came out to show us, just as someone was coming in, seeing Ruth, she exclaimed, "She looks beautiful." We heartily agreed. Everybody loves a wedding and Ruth's was no exception, a very pretty wedding on a wonderful July day, everyone enjoyed it, and everything went like clockwork. Not surprising with the father of the bride a clergyman!

Paul was now working in Germany and although he had girlfriends was not really interested in any particular girl. We visited him on more than one occasion, and when he lived in the Black Forest area he introduced us to St Ursula's, Freiburg, and to St Nicholas, Basle, our first overseas contact with the Intercontinental Church Society. We realised the necessity for English speaking Churches in Europe. Paul travelled many miles to get to Church and we were so pleased he was keeping up his contacts in this way. He became interested in skiing and later, with this interest in mind went to the Schloss Mittersil, in Austria. From all he has said, this is a great place for young people, with skiing, Bible study and Christian fellowship, it had much to offer - and still does I hope! There he met a young girl, Anna. Born in Finland, she joined the houseparty with friends from Sweden, where she now lived with her family. They formed a group and sang together, going their separate ways after the holiday. Some years later, while working in Switzerland,

Paul was sent to Sweden by his company. He found his way to the International Church in Stockholm, and there met up with Anna again, but this time it was different, as his letters and phone calls soon told us.

That year we had planned to visit Paul in his flat outside of Bern, where he worked. To to our delight, Anna came over for a weekend, and because Paul was working, Hugh went to the station to meet her. We had seen pictures of Anna, and as he looked at the passengers alighting from the train, he spotted her. So, going up to this young girl, he asked, "Are you Anna?" She answered, "Yes, hello Dad." Dear Anna, she made our family complete. We have always been so happy with Paul's choice of a wife, even if he did take quite a time finding her!

Their wedding was a remarkable affair! It took place in Sweden in January, but we had sunshine and a reasonable temperature. The Stockholm International Church Anna attended had a large Conference Centre; church members also used this for holidays during the summer, a beautiful spot on the Baltic coast, about twenty miles out of the city. Because it was out of season, they were able to hold the wedding there.

Along with Ruth, Mark and their small family, we were joined by Martin and Robert and some of Paul's friends from the church he had attended at Christ Church, Cockfosters. We were able to meet Anna's parents and family and see the beautiful wedding dress, made by Anna's mother. Our one problem was no common language. The civil ceremony had to be in Swedish, but the wedding service was in Finnish, led by Anna's family's home pastor, and English, taken by Hugh. One Scandinavian custom we thought delightful was included. Before the service started, Anna's mother, Tertu, and I each lit a candle on a small table at the front of the large lounge where the ceremony was held, and then, after exchanging vows and rings. Paul and Anna lit one large candle from the other two, which they then extinguished. A beautiful symbolic action! The reception was very enjoyable too, with many participating in humorous and varied musical items. Some of the guests were in national costume, both Swedish and Finnish, a very colourful sight. Paul prepared, with Anna's help, a short speech in Finnish!

The day after the wedding we went to the morning service at the International Church in Stockholm, we were amazed at the set-up. A six-storey corner block, with a hotel and restaurant and shops underneath, and even a Police Station within the complex. We were shown workrooms for woodwork, photography and weaving, also a sports hall, to name but a few of the activities people became involved in on these premises, in addition to the facilities for Christian worship. This took place in three separate areas, and in three different languages, Swedish, English - with an American accent! - and Korean! We understood that there were eight pastors involved in all. The workrooms were spotless, I commented on the fact that in the woodwork room there was no sawdust, and was shown a huge extractor fan that did not even allow the sawdust to settle. This church was really reaching out into the community in so many directions - we were most impressed.

We went by lift to the English speaking Church and in this completely self contained area we found tables and chairs set out for young children to sit with their parents, so that they could paint or draw while the service was on. Going down three steps we came to the main part of the worship area. We much enjoyed the service, led by a young American pastor, and afterwards over coffee chatted to many of our fellow worshippers.

Arriving back at the Conference house we had lunch and Hugh and I went for a walk. Coming back, I slipped on some black ice, and broke my wrist.

The warden and his wife were wonderful, and before we knew what was happening I was at the local hospital, as an emergency, having my wrist set, and it was not 24 hours after Paul and Anna's wedding!

On our return we wondered if the rest of the family knew what had happened. It was quiet, probably they were out for a walk. The door opened and Ruth and Mark and the family came in, looking anxious, but pleased to see I could still smile. Jonny came running up to me, (he has big brown eyes, just like Paul's) and taking my good hand in his he said, "Granny 'ulbert, you 'ave 'urt your 'and, I will 'elp you, I will 'old your 'and." With comfort and help like that, I knew all would be well. The amusing thing is that when he was just over three Jonny found it difficult to pronounce his "H's", and because of this I will never forget his love and concern for me that day. Later Ruth and Mark told us as soon as he heard granny had hurt her arm he said "Let us talk to Jesus about it." "Train a child in the way he should go and he will not depart from it."

But to take up my story again about our time in Worthing. One morning I discovered a lump in my breast, and went to my doctor who made an appointment for me to see a consultant at Worthing Hospital. This proved to be a severe case of mastitis and I was eventually given a clean bill of health. Such a relief to us all, we were so thankful.

About six months later, however, I noticed another lump, but did not go to my GP immediately, thinking that like the other one, it would go away, but it did not. After a week or so I saw doctor, who made an appointment for me to see the consultant again. I had quite a wait and thought it must be all right, they would see me sooner if there was a need, but the lump did not go away and was getting bigger. One morning I had a telephone call from the hospital saying they had a cancellation for the afternoon clinic, could I be there by 2.30 pm, I said "Yes." Talking to patients waiting to see the consultant that day, I realised I was not the only one with a 2.30 pm appointment, and prepared myself for a long wait.

As I feared, I was told I had cancer of the breast and would need surgery. The hospital would be in touch with me later.

We could not believe it. Having breast-fed three children, I believed this was a good preventative against breast cancer. But it was happening to me and I felt fearful for the future.

I was asked to be at the hospital by 10 am on the last Sunday in November 1979. As Hugh was involved with services, Mark took me in. I did not get a bed until after 2.30 pm, a long wait, but I had a good lunch and chatted with a lady also waiting for a bed, and due to have the same operation. We had adjoining beds and had surgery the same day.

Before leaving hospital I was asked if I would agree to Radiology. Not knowing much about it, I agreed. The doctor said, "With the surgery it will give you 100% protection, and will kill off any remaining cancer cells." They said they would be in touch about treatment later, when I was feeling stronger.

A friend paid for me to have two weeks' convalescence in the Mildmay Convalescent Home, about five minutes walk from the vicarage. Such a blessing, it got me on my feet again. Every evening, Mildmay had a short evening service, nothing heavy, just a quiet, peaceful time of worship. Some of our own congregation were involved and I much appreciated their ministry. It was great to see them sharing in this caring work. The regular pianist was Peggy, who was a near neighbour of ours, and was very gifted musically. She had a gentle, quiet way with her and I know God used her greatly in the home.

About six weeks later I started a three-week course of Radiotherapy at the Royal Sussex Hospital, Brighton. Leaving Worthing just after eight in the morning, we were picked up by a minibus, collecting more patients en route. The minibus had to wait until all the patients had finished treatment before taking them home. As I was on two different machines, and therefore had to join two different queues, my treatment took quite a time. I usually got home between 1 and 2 pm completely exhausted. The treatment was not painful, but the accumulative effects of the radium on one's body brought problems. However, we were all the same, and learned that cancer is no respecter of persons, it is a great leveller.

As we waited for our turn, we chatted and got to know each other, the staff were very friendly and did all they could to help us. After treatment, if there was time, we went to the canteen, where they made a good cup of tea, and had interesting cakes for sale. I discovered they made the most delicious Bovril, with granules, but I've never found it in the shops - pity!

At the end of the second week, I developed a severe pain problem and had to see the doctor. He stopped treatment for a day, and gave me painkillers. As this was on a Friday, I had the weekend to let things settle down. The following Monday morning Hugh decided to take me to Brighton in our car. That week we arrived at the hospital early, and as there was only a short queue I was seen quickly, and left before the minibus arrived. Using our car was so much more comfortable and I was so grateful to my dear husband.

Somewhere near the hospital was a homemade cake shop selling delicious, fattening cream cakes, and most of us needed to put weight on! At the end of treatment, patients enjoyed the ritual of going to the shop and choosing a gooey cream cake to celebrate the end of RT and we knew we deserved it! At the beginning of treatment we were told to eat wholesome food, with a good intake of dairy produce, get plenty of rest, but not to let water get anywhere near the area of our body being treated.

A heavy dose of radium makes one very tired. We were given special cream to use before we started to blister, and another cream to apply once the blisters started. When the "cooking time" was completed, the hospital would make an appointment to see us in outpatients.

Dorothea, a friend, rang asking for my help. A near neighbour, a lady of about fifty, was dying of cancer. She was at home. The doctor who had treated me at the Royal Sussex visited her one evening. Talking with Ann and her husband, he said to her, "I'm sorry, there is nothing more I can do, you are living on borrowed time." Not an easy thing to say, I knew he was a very caring man and was deeply concerned for his patients. We all had a great respect for him. Later, Ann said, first to her husband, and then to her friend, "I want to know how to meet my God, what must I do?"

It was at this point that Dorothea rang me, asking if I could visit Ann and talk about it. My answer was a loud "No".

I said to Hugh, "This is too close. The same cancer, surgery, and treatment, the same doctor, and in less than two years, Ann is dying. I can't do it." What would you have said?

My friend rang a few days later, saying, "Ann is deteriorating and has not got long to live, your circumstances are so similar, I'm sure you can help her, will you change your mind?" Again I said," No, surely there is someone else who could help her." But Dorothea was adamant, I was the one.

But I could not get Ann out of my mind and said to God, "I cannot go, you know how I feel, it's too much, don't ask me to do this." Very gently and quietly, I was aware of something inside me saying, "You can, I will help you." Was this really what God wanted me to do? I told Hugh and he said I should contact Dorothea.

That morning I saw Ann, but I don't think she could actually see me. Her first words were, "Grace, how can I prepare to meet my God?" In a few words I told her.

Hugh has just read these paragraphs, and his comment is: "What did you say to Ann?" Again, he is right, and I respect his insight.

All I said was, "Ann, ask the Lord Jesus to forgive your sins and thank Him for dying for you, and tell him you love Him." "Is that all?" she asked. I answered, "Yes." After a short time Ann said, "I'm ready to meet my God now."

Dorothea told us later that Ann's brother had been praying for her for many years. When he next walked into the house, he stopped, just inside the front door, and said, "What has happened, the atmosphere in the house has completely changed?" On being told Ann had made her peace with God and was His child, he was full of thanksgiving and praise to the Lord for answering his prayer.

Our belief is so simple, it confounds the wise and learned at times, and yet it is so easy to understand, that someone as ill as Ann, knew, in less than five minutes, that she was prepared to meet her God.

By the time my appointment to see the consultant came, I was looking and feeling much better, it was good to see friends, especially from the Royal Sussex days, showing great improvement, we had much to talk about while we waited our turn.

About two days later I was in such pain, I saw my GP. He prescribed painkillers, and after a week or so, the pain wore off and I felt better. My next appointment at the hospital, some months later, produced the same effect, about two days later I was in great pain. Again I saw my GP and a further appointment was made for me to see a consultant. By the time I saw him, I was feeling much better. On examining me, he made arrangements for further tests. Two days or so later, I was in pain once more. We began to see a pattern of pain two days after each hospital appointment. The tests proved clear, the pain went and I began to live a normal life again. The next appointment produced the same results, more pain. I had more tests, thankfully showing no cancer, but the pain was getting more persistent and lasting longer. My doctor gave me all the support he could; I saw various consultants but did not get satisfactory answers, as far as pain was concerned. As all the tests proved clear, I came to the conclusion that I was one of the most cancer free people in Worthing, but the problem of pain persisted. I began to think this was to be a way of life and tried to live accordingly, but it was not easy.

We had a Missionary weekend and the joy of entertaining two nurses working with leprosy patients. Hugh and I decided not to refer to my problem. After a meal, Hugh left us chatting, while he did some things in the study. One of them said, "Grace you are in pain, what is wrong?" I replied, "How do you know?" She answered, "Your eyes tell us, we see the same look of pain in the eyes of our leprosy patients. We think you may have a nerve problem."

So far, I have only talked about pain after examinations, because it was almost unbearable, but it's true to say, I was always in some pain and anything could start if off. Bending down to pick up my grandchildren or even holding them caused pain; sitting in the pews during a service, putting washing on the line, sitting in a car. Someone gave me a pat on the back, and although very gentle, it made me see stars! But this was not severe and after a day or so subsided to a normal level. After one examination, Hugh sent for the doctor. Our own GP was away and another doctor came. After examining me, he said, "You have shingles on the scar line, and will come out in a rash later." Yet no rash appeared. That was when we decided I should take painkillers after examination, lie down and wait for the pain to subside to bearable level, usually in a day or two. Sorry to go on about this, but this problem was one we could not ignore.

Our people were caring and supportive and I, knowing I was surrounded by prayer, hid my feelings as much as possible, but pain was always in the background of my life, ready to pounce if I did anything to annoy it!

We had enjoyed our parish in Worthing and had many encouragements, but after surgery, I felt I was holding back and not pulling my weight. Because I had worked alongside Hugh for over twenty-five years, and had not gone out to work myself, this was very hard to bear. With two churches, and everything in duplicate, we found our time together was limited and sometimes the "day off" was nonexistent. In so many ways the pressure was on.

Hugh was busy, I was in pain. We prayed about the matter and decided to make an appointment to see our Bishop and talk things over with him.

The Bishop was very kind and understanding. A little while after our meeting we had a letter from him, asking if Hugh would consider an appointment as priest-in-charge of Holy Trinity, Hove. This was what is called a Conventional District, within the parish of All Saints, but a church with an evangelical tradition and a small vicarage. He said he would get in touch with the churchwardens and we could take it from there.

From the beginning, we had both thought that Hugh would remain in Worthing until retirement and were grieved now that things were not working out as we had hoped and planned.

CHAPTER 10
HOVE, HAILSHAM AND RETIREMENT

We met the wardens', Arthur and John, with Alfred, the lay reader at Holy Trinity, Hove, and felt very much at one with them. Talking about the parish, its work and outreach, it became clear this was our sort of place. I left Hugh discussing parochial affairs and looked around the church, a fine well kept building. The flowers were beautifully arranged and looked so welcoming. Indeed the whole atmosphere gave me a gentle welcome. A lady came from the choir vestry and introduced herself as Barbara, again, that feeling of welcome, we just "clicked".

I was impressed with all I saw and heard, but there was one problem. Before leaving Worthing I had asked God to confirm things, as far as I was concerned, by letting me see some grass from the kitchen window, for some strange reason this was very important to me. I did not say how much, or make any other request. At Worthing, my view from the kitchen had been the boundary wall and the side wall of the house next door. We both felt there was a reluctance to show us the vicarage and wondered why. It looked small, but with our children now away from home, this was not a problem. Seeing round the house, we realised just how small it was, but were told of plans to extend the kitchen and build a new dining room. I went over to the kitchen window and pulled the curtain aside and saw a grass patch, with rather overgrown bushes needing attention. But I could see grass from the kitchen window! God had granted my request, the only one I have ever made regarding our accommodation.

We said goodbye and made our way back to Worthing, rather quiet in the car, thinking of all we had seen and heard. If you have read this far, you will know that as soon as we got home, we prayed about the whole matter, and both felt sure Hove would be our next sphere of work.

Bidding farewell to our many friends in Worthing was not easy; the thought of leaving them pulled my heartstrings. It's just the way I'm made I suppose. Their Christian maturity and love is something I still treasure. Together we had shared in the "fellowship of the gospel". We were "bundles of life", tied together with cords of love, a precious gift from God.

Making our way along the coast on moving day, we knew the only reason for leaving was my problem of pain, the result of cancer, and after two years or more, I was no nearer finding an answer to it.

As we settled into our new home and got to know the congregation, that warm feeling of welcome was still evident. Leaving a big vicarage and going small meant that we could not take all our furniture, a good thing really, it meant less to clean.

We did not talk about my problem in the parish, but Barbara, who had been a nurse, soon realised things were not easy for me.

Ruth and Mark, along with Rachel, two months old, spent Christmas with us our first year in Hove. It was lovely to have a baby in the house again, especially at such a wonderful time. They had a kitten, and we said they could bring it with them, no problem. One morning, as I was having my cup of tea in bed, the kitten jumped up on me, putting his paws on the scar as he landed. In a day or so, I was in pain, and could still feel the place where the kitten had landed on me. It was a strange feeling, so off I went to the doctor. He was very understanding and said, "You could have Cat Scratch fever"! Odd name, but that's what he said! Asking if he could examine me, but realising I was afraid to be touched, he said, "It is necessary, I will be very gentle." He was, and at first it seemed as though I was getting away with it. But two days after it was the same story, pain with a vengeance. We sent for doctor, who ordered me to bed and said he would do tests and prescribed painkillers and other tablets. Barbara was wonderful, we were so thankful to have her help. I felt awful, in bed so soon after our arrival at Hove, but it could not be helped.

All my tests were clear, but just in case I had a scan once I was up and about. The X-ray department was getting to know me by this time. The appointment was on Hugh's birthday. Not a very exciting thing to do on one's birthday, take your wife to hospital, especially as there was a four hour wait between having the injection and the actual scan. I had to drink four pints of fluid during that four hours. But every cloud has a silver lining - I was told right away, "There is no malignancy, you are clear." As I said to Hugh afterwards, "That is the best birthday present I have ever given you." He readily agreed!

After this storm in a teacup, my doctor said, "Don't let anyone examine you again, they have others ways of finding out if anything is wrong." I was greatly relieved.

I got back into the swing of things in the parish, taking the Women's Fellowship, visiting and getting to know the congregation. During the week we held an evening Bible study in the vicarage and a time for prayer, in the church hall, each Tuesday morning. Terry and Sue ran the Overseas Missionary Fellowship monthly prayer meeting; so there was quite a bit going on, as there is in most parishes of course.

One Tuesday morning I noticed that Mrs Yeomans, a lady of about 97 years, was wearing a new pair of black patent shoes. I passed some comment and she said, in her deep voice, "Well my dear, it's important to look nice, even if you are getting on a bit!" She always called me 'My dear' and was a real character. Ken went to her house and collected her for church twice on a Sunday, and did any odd jobs that needed doing. When I visited her one day she looked at the clock and said, "Four- o-clock, time to feed the birds, my dear, I always feed them at four, they're used to it, I don't like to disappoint them." I noticed a seed tray doing very well on a table in the garden, and asked her what they were. She answered, "Stocks, I like them and always plant up some for the summer." Any spare time she had was spent knitting bed jackets. She must have made dozens. Anyone going into hospital was given a bed jacket. If you were ill at home, a bed jacket, wrapped in a brown paper bag made its way to your front door. She would say, "You can have white, blue or pink." It was the custom for the Mayor of Hove to attend Holy Trinity on the first Sunday morning of the New Year. If he had a wife, she was given a bed jacket, wrapped in brown paper.

Mrs Yeomans lived to be over 100 years old. She had a Guinness every day and said, "That's what keeps me going my dear!" A truly remarkable lady!

Dudley, the organist has played at Holy Trinity for over fifty years, and only misses if he is on holiday, and is seldom ill. He is quite a character. Hugh and I have had some delicious meals at his home, cooked by his wife Margaret. She is so supportive of all he does, they are a grand pair. (Quite recently Dudley was called home to be with his Lord - he is very much missed.)

Margery and Edna hosted a Monday evening prayer time in their home. As former nurses, they kept an eye on the older folk, and if anyone was ill, would quickly offer help. They always had a deep sense of fun and Christian joy; doing the patient as much good as any medicine prescribed by the doctor. They were so hospitable and showed practical Christianity with a smile, they were certainly "given to hospitality."

Trudie was well known for her apple pies. Now over eighty years old, she had come over from Germany at the end of the war and never really lost her accent. She was a warm, friendly character and I'm quite sure her apple pies opened many doors for her. She would knock on the front door and hand you a greaseproof bag, saying, "I thought you would like this." They were delicious. She once told me, "I make the pastry with butter." Walking along the road with her could take a long time, as she was always stopping to say hello to her many friends and passing the time of day with them.

Iris moved into the parish just after we arrived, and before long was busy helping Hugh in the study with secretarial work which was very much appreciated. Visiting her one afternoon, as we chatted over a cup of tea, she said, "Grace, I've not really settled here, I don't know what to do." To my amazement, I replied, "Get out of this flat." My answer surprised us both; the flat was excellent, nothing wrong with it. I apologised. "I'm sorry, I should not have said that." But Iris replied, "You are right, I had not realised it before, but it's true, I must get out of this flat." Thinking about it since has made me realise I was not at ease in the flat, but I have no idea why. As Iris said, "I don't know what to do", I knew, deep inside me, the flat was the problem, not Iris.

Doreen was a gracious, charming lady who somehow made everything "special". Such people are the backbone of any church, the salt of the earth, and how we thank God for them. There are so many I have not mentioned, this would be impossible, they are just ordinary people, but all loving and serving their extraordinary God.

Alfred, the lay reader was a delightful man, he had a charisma about him. With his wife Daphne, he took early retirement, bought a bungalow nearby and together they became very much involved with the life of the church. Sadly, before we arrived, Daphne died of cancer, and although he missed her greatly Alfred carried on. House group meetings in his lovely bungalow near the road to Devil's Dyke were wonderful times of fellowship. Sometime later he was very unwell and the local hospital diagnosed cancer. After treatment, he went into remission for about six months, and during this time he preached some remarkable sermons. It seemed as though he had had a glimpse of heaven during his illness and had to pass it on. We all missed him greatly when he died; everybody loved him.

Willie Oelsner, was a Lutheran pastor, and a German with some Jewish ancestry. Bishop Bell of Chichester, got him over to this country just before the war, and later he was ordained in the Anglican church. He was invited to Holy Trinity, Hove, where he stayed for over twenty years and had a very loving and effective ministry, before retiring to Malvern. Like Trudie, he never lost his accent. We met him when he returned to Hove after his wife's death, and very much enjoyed our association with him.

The planned extension began to take shape. Terry, mentioned earlier in connection with the OMF, was our own architect and, because he knew the house, produced a really good extension plan that fulfilled all our expectations, and provided a delightfully easy home to live in.

The kitchen was completely gutted, it was utter chaos, but it did not bother us, the end result was what we kept in mind. We were invited out to meals, that is why I knew we had some very good cooks in the parish, and we had great times of fellowship around the meal table.

At last the work was finished, the painters put the last dab of paint on and I started to clean up. It was a Friday evening, Hugh had gone over to the Church Hall for the Men's Fellowship. Just before coffee time, Alfred popped over to see how things were going, and invited me to coffee, and I was only too ready to stop. The painters had made the fanlight windows their last job and left saying, "Leave the windows open until you go to bed tonight, they should be dry by then." During coffee we talked about the extension and I invited the men to come over afterwards and look around. Hugh was talking to someone, and then he turned to me, saying, "I've got something in the study that would be useful, I'll go and get it." At the end of the Men's Fellowship we all walked over to inspect the work, going in by the new utility room side door, and being men they were very interested and had a good look at everything. Hugh noticed a strange mark on the newly painted window sill, but no one had an answer as to what it could be.

After the men went, we shut all the windows, and as he looked at the mark on the sill Hugh said, "It could have been made by a heel", but we agreed it would need to be a small, slim person to make an entry through the fanlight. As we started going upstairs, Hugh said, "You stay down here, if anyone did get into the house, they could still be upstairs." I thought it very unlikely, but did as I was told, and got a broom from the cupboard, calling up to Hugh, "If anyone is in the house I'll go for them with the broom as they come down the stairs."

All was quiet and I wondered what was going on, still standing with my broom at the bottom of the stairs. It seemed an age before Hugh came to the top of the stairs and said, "Darling, we have been burgled." Leaving my broom, I rushed upstairs into our bedroom. There on the bed were the individual cases that had contained all my most precious family jewellery. Presents from my father to my mother, a valuable broach from a friend, a beautiful pendant my mother-in-law had been given as a little girl. I felt so sad and hurt inside as I looked at the lovely, old-fashioned boxes and realised I would not see their contents again!

Hugh rang the police, but there was little they could do. However they did say, "When the Vicar came into the house, he probably disturbed the burglar, and it was fortunate he was not attacked." That was our one consolation, but I was very unhappy inside and could not get it off my mind.

We got to bed late that night, both of us suffering from shock as we thought of someone getting into our home and doing such a thing. If you have been burgled, you will know how we felt. The sin of such an action leaves pain, sadness and distress.

The police came again on Saturday morning, but said, "There is little we can do, it is unlikely you will see your jewellery again." We accepted that fact, but inside, I was still so sad.

On Sunday morning, Hugh was over in the church, I was doing things in the kitchen and can remember my thoughts very clearly and the spot where God dealt with me. I was praying a whining, grumbling prayer, "Lord, why did you let this happen, you know those things were precious to me and can never be replaced, I feel so awful, you must help me." And then I heard a voice inside me say, "But you're safe, aren't you?" I just stood still, stopped what I was doing and said, "Thank you Lord, I'm so sorry, please forgive me, thank you for keeping Hugh safe." As I prayed that prayer my heart was overwhelmed with thanksgiving and praise and I vowed to God that, "I will never allow things to become so important to me again - things are not vital to me - Hugh is."

I was wearing my engagement ring and a ring a friend had given me. The next time I got a suit out of the wardrobe I saw a broach on the lapel of the jacket. It had blue stones and a pearl surround, and had been my mother-in-law's. She had worn it a lot and we were both pleased it had not been taken.

Hugh has just read the foregoing paragraphs and he remarked, "You're laying it on a bit thick aren't you?" Maybe I am, but it's true. When I started writing this book I gave a chapter to Adrian Plass, and said, "Please would you help me and read this through and tell me what you think." I got a typically AP reply. "Write the truth, describe what you feel, so that your reader (if this ever gets published, my comment!) knows all that went on inside you." Having read many of his books I have come to the conclusion that Adrian writes from 'inside' - 'outside' - a gift from God

Going for my 'check ups' at the hospital, I always made a point of saying I could not be examined, and explained why! This caused no problem, until one day a doctor said, "No, I must examine you." Explaining my problem of pain after examination, I said this was not possible, my notes would explain. But the doctor would not accept this. And I could not possibly allow it. There was no way through. I was told that unless I agreed to the request it was pointless attending the outpatients' clinic. As any cancer patient knows, one attends the clinic for a certain number of years and then hopefully gets the 'all clear'. A day of great rejoicing! With all my problems, I still had a year to complete the time. I remember saying, "Do you know what you are doing? I cannot agree to your request." The reply was: "Unless you do, don't made another appointment to come to this clinic." Sitting on the chair, facing the doctor, I could hardly believe my ears; it seemed so cruel. Because no one had diagnosed the reason for the pain, in my mind, this doctor was ignoring my problem, just as though it was not there. Probably thought it was all in my mind, I don't know, but as I got up from the chair and walked out of the consulting room my world collapsed. The above is not word perfect, that's not possible, but is as I remember. One does not like writing such things, but it is the truth and part of my story.

Hugh was in the waiting room and as I told him all that had happened, my tears started. I walked past the appointment area, we got into the car and drove home. I hoped the hospital would ring asking why I had not made my next appointment. No phone call came. I wondered what the doctor had put on my notes.

My tears still came, at any time, unbidden. What was wrong with me! I went to my doctor, he was on holiday, but I saw a lady doctor. She was very understanding and prescribed something to help me. My great worry was that if I had any further cancer I could not go to that hospital. What would I do? I know now that other hospitals would have been open to me, but then it seemed like the end of the world. I was in a kind of no-man's land, with pain the hospital could not treat, or even try to understand. A friend I first met in Worthing Hospital had died, some of the people I got to know during treatment had died, I was alive, but at times it seemed only just. Was it my turn next?

In any illness pain is likely to be a problem, and I have stressed the pain I felt after examination, but to a certain degree, I was always in pain. Anything could trigger it off. Holding anything too heavy, I could not pick up my grandchildren, or sit them on my lap, in case they pressed against me. Someone patted my back, and I saw stars. Shopping, cleaning, sitting on certain chairs, sitting in pews, increased the pain that was always in the background. I grew to live with it and accepted it as a way of life, but the pain after examination was unbearable. All I could do was take the prescribed tablets, and wait for the pain to ease.

Such a story was bound to get around to some of the congregation, and those who heard it were very sympathetic. One lady was most concerned and asked if she could pay for me to see a consultant privately. This thought had never entered my head and I gladly accepted. When the doctor saw me, he suggested I examined myself, stopping when I felt a change in my reaction, he was surprised at the area affected and suggested I saw a pain consultant. At last we were getting somewhere!

109

We could no longer cope with busy parish life, so we contacted the Bishop. Having been left some money, and with help from the Church of England Pensions Board, we had bought a house in Hailsham for our retirement. Hugh asked if it was possible for him to retire early, before he reached 65 years old, so that my life would be less demanding. The Bishop was very understanding and said he would be in touch when he had looked into the matter.

After a few weeks, I had a phone call from a hospital saying, "We have made an appointment for you to see a pain consultant in six months time." Sitting at Hugh's desk (Douglas) to take the call, I said, "Six months! I cannot possibly wait that long, is there no way round this?" The person on the other end of the line said, "You could go privately, I have the doctor's telephone number, would you like it?" I checked with Hugh, as to whether we could afford to go privately on such an unknown matter. My wonderful husband replied, "Whatever it costs to free you from this pain, we will and can afford it."

I rang the number; the doctor's secretary answered. When I explained my problem, she said, "That's all right, when would you like an appointment?" I said, "As soon as possible." "Would Friday do?" she replied. I answered with a very grateful, "Yes please". This was Tuesday afternoon.

I rang my doctor with the news, he was pleased something was being done, but did warn me, "The specialist will probably ask you some strange questions." My reply was, "I don't care what he asks me, as long as we get rid of the pain."

Pain control is much more to the front of patients' needs now. Research has made great progress in this area. The work of MacMillan Nurses, and the Hospice movement have helped so much in pain control. I for one am very thankful.

We saw the doctor together, he asked questions, but did not attempt to examine me. Then, after asking about my last appointment at hospital he said, "Please could you give me the name of the doctor you saw last time you attended the outpatients' clinic." I heard myself saying, "No, I cannot do

110

that." The doctor asked if I remembered the name, although he must have known I would never forget it. He then tried another tactic saying, "You don't want other patients to be treated like this, do you?" Again a, "No, but if you really want the doctor's name, all you have to do is check up on my last appointment, I cannot give it to you."

"Forgive us our sins, as we forgive those who sin against us." I had no bitterness in my heart, I had truly forgiven what to me, had been a great injustice. I was free. Until then, I had had no idea how firmly ingrained this teaching was in me.

While all this was going on in my mind I heard doctor say, "I can help you, but it will mean going into a private hospital nearby, and making use of their operating room and using drugs. I cannot do anything about that, but I will not take my own fee."

I went into hospital the following Tuesday for treatment, one week after ringing the secretary. After three weeks, I visited doctor again and we arranged another appointment at the hospital. Again a three weeks' wait, to let things settle down, then another appointment. I was feeling the difference in my body, it was wonderful to be losing pain. I asked doctor what he was doing. He explained that my nerves had become broken, and he injected a jelly substance into the broken ends so that they were no longer rubbing each other and then the pain went. I know doctor dealt with a least fifteen nerve ends. No wonder I had been in such pain.

Waiting for the secretary to open the doctor's front door one day, I looked up and saw a mezuzah attached to the door post and realised the doctor was a Jew. I thanked God for all the kindness, skill, and generosity shown to me by one of his children.

By this time our kind Bishop had set things in motion and Hugh was invited to join the staff at St Mary's Hailsham as an assistant minister, until he reached retirement age in about eighteen months time. He had already met the Vicar, Roger Porthouse, and felt confident that this would be a good arrangement. We knew that this was God's planning for our present circumstances so we reluctantly said goodbye to the folk at Hove and moved to our house at Hailsham at the beginning of 1986. The plan worked well, some of our friends agreed that this was a good way into retirement. One clergy wife said she was dreading retirement: one day her husband would be the vicar, the next day he would be sitting in the pew, an ordinary person with no responsibilities. She knew he would not find this easy.

And so, into retirement, after nearly 37 years of ministry together. We had six months off, had a good holiday, saw the families and friends and enjoyed doing nothing. The first Easter weekend after retirement, all the family went to the Methodist Holiday Home in Swanage. Paul having recently returned from a skiing holiday in Austria, came with a broken ankle, on crutches. We had a wonderful time, the weather was unusually warm, the children could swim and paddle. This was the first time we had been together as a complete family. Vicki and Rachel wrote notes to all the guests wishing them a Happy Easter, and slid them under the doors. We had walks, chatted, read and relaxed and enjoyed our wonderful family.

The Intercontinental Church Society asked Hugh if he, like other retired but still active clergymen would be interested in a SAGA holiday chaplaincy. We were, and in the following three years enjoyed visits to Minorca and two resorts on the Spanish mainland. We soon realised how hard the chaplain had to work. We usually found the SAGA representatives very helpful, but sometimes had to battle a bit to get a room or lounge, or part of a dining hall to use for a Sunday service. Other groups such as those playing bingo and cards often seemed to think that they had a prior claim! However, we met some great people, saw some interesting places, but were always glad to get home again!

CHAPTER 11
BASLE AND TUNIS

With Paul and Anna living just outside of Bern, Switzerland, we were only too pleased to say yes when the Intercontinental Church Society asked Hugh if he would consider doing a locum chaplaincy in the English speaking Church in Basle. This was to be for about eight weeks from the middle of January 1992. We had visited the church with Paul some years previously, while he was living in Freiburg. Paul had attended the monthly services held at St Ursula's, taken by the Basle chaplain, Tom Roberts, and had often travelled in to worship at Basle on Sunday evenings. Now we are in the Common Market we know the work of ICS is even more vital to the English-speaking people on the Continent. We have never been called overseas, but are pleased that in retirement, we have been able to take part in the work of a missionary society we had supported in the parishes.

We had such a warm welcome from the church members and I still remember Gillian's help with shopping at the local Migros the first morning of our stay. We did not take the car, but found that the tram and train services were excellent and always on time, and were most impressed. We lived in an upstairs flat in Church House, the ground floor rooms being used for meetings. We were very comfortable and soon got used to the Swiss way of doing things. Of course during our stay Paul and Anna visited us from Bern with their lovely dog, Bella. She is another golden retriever, we always said she was a distant cousin of Dexter's!

The church folk were friendly, hospitable and appreciative, it was a pleasure to serve them. Their homes were so different to ours, and everyone used a car or tram to get to church, because they lived so far away. At the time I am writing about, the English congregation was able to use St Nicholas in the city centre for an early Communion and an evening service, while other nationalities used the church during the day. To be the minister of a congregation, with no actual church building, and

113

having to find the right place for worship, on a good tram route, and fitting in with the times the building was free, called for great wisdom. I missed the Church of England parochial system.

While we were at Basle, Jonathan Gibbs visited Switzerland with a view to becoming the next permanent chaplain. We met his wife Toni and their little daughter Harriet, and both of us felt they were the right people for this work and were delighted to hear later that Jonathan had accepted the chaplaincy. We still receive the newsletter and follow the work with much prayer and interest.

This morning we received the current ICS Magazine with its prayer diary. I quote from the section referring to Basle:

"Morning prayer now takes place in the Pauluskirche. Pray that the congregation will put the new facilities to good use and will find effective ways to reach out to friends and acquaintances."

This bears out my comments in a previous paragraph about the need for sensitivity in choosing a place of worship for the Anglican Church in Basle. We know that family services are now an important part of worship, and are so encouraged that the church is growing.

As with any church, one starts with those who attend and we found a delightfully mixed bag in the congregation. Since the Church house was some distance from the city centre, we were very glad to have the help of Emmie, with her little red car, and have reason to say "Thank you" for the many lifts she gave us. I have mentioned Gillian, who was so practical and helpful throughout our stay. She took us through the intricacies of getting oil for Church house. We had a meal at her home and met the family, and are still in touch. One cannot leave "Frankie" out, a great character, much involved with all that went on in the church. She was in England when the war started and could not return home until hostilities ceased, and so joined our Land Army. Her English was very good, and she had a real love for our people, and was happy to worship with the English speaking church in Basle.

Brian and Joy were great stalwarts of the church, always available whenever there was a need. We discovered that Joy was a wonderful cook, and had some delicious meals in their house. Brian's work was involved with rail transport and he travelled all over the world. Just over a year ago, he was made redundant, but this turned out to be a blessing in disguise. He went for a check-up and discovered he had cancer, but typical of Brian, he took this in a very positive way, My last information of him was that all was well, and he was praising and thanking God that the cancer had been discovered at the check up.

Roger was another interesting person. He asked me if I knew the "Grace Magazine", his father was the editor. In reply I said, "Yes I discovered it a few years ago, and I find it a helpful, useful magazine." Roger was good at befriending newcomers; we saw this gift used when a "refugee" contacted us and came along to the services. One of our great joys in Basle was to see this dear man reverently holding a Bible, printed in his own language, and joining with us in Bible study.

Gordon and Sarah were a delightfully practical couple and so supportive. Gordon edited the newsletter and Sarah helped in the Sunday school. All the time we were in Basle, we were aware of their influence on the life of the Church.

We have grown to love Switzerland. The mountains and lakes, the wonderful castles and restaurants, sometimes perched high up on the mountains, but never falling off! No litter, everything running like clockwork. Their English is very good, their cooking excellent, and they are so hospitable. But I did miss the English sense of humour and everything was very expensive, and believe it or not, we missed the "British banger"! We made more than one mistake with the "Swiss sausage!" But one cannot have everything. It's a wonderful country! They could teach us so much. Perhaps I'm especially thinking of trains at the moment. From Doctor Beeching onwards, one can see a gradual decline in services in this country, but not in costs! The Swiss make full use of their trains and buses: they are on time, cheap and do not pollute the atmosphere!

Hugh had his seventieth birthday while we were there. It was on a Sunday, and, to his great delight, he was able to preach in two countries on his birthday. In the morning at St Ursula's, Freiburg, in Germany, and at night at St Nicholas, Basle, in Switzerland. After the evening service we went to a restaurant frequented by the congregation. I had told them it was Hugh's birthday and after we had enjoyed our hot chocolate, coffee, soup or what have you, they presented him with a cake! I cannot remember who made it, but it was delicious, and Hugh was thrilled.

This was our last Sunday, before going for a short holiday at the Hotel Edelweiss, on Lake Brienz, run by Priscilla and Ron. We had a few days enjoying the wonderful countryside and making good use of the steamers on the lake. A must for us was the Kleine Scheidegg, our special mountain. We had a meal outside enjoying the winter sunshine and sat admiring the absolute beauty of God's creation. The memory is still with me, a perfect end to our chaplaincy in Basle.

After a few weeks at home, we heard from ICS, asking if Hugh would like to go to Tunis for six weeks. St George's, Tunis was also without a Chaplain. This really exercised us in prayer, we had never been to that part of the world and we knew it was a Muslim country, quite a different proposition from Basle. We consulted our dear friends from St John's Deptford days, Don and Mary Churchman, who had recently returned from Tunis and were able to give us information about the chaplaincy, as indeed they had already done in the case of Basle. We felt that the need constituted the call. Hugh wrote to ICS saying we were willing to go. This would be from the middle of May to the end of June, with very hot weather. We went to the charity shops searching for 100% cotton clothing, but this was not easy to find, although we did get some shirts and blouses. The thought of this chaplaincy really excited us, as we would be breaking new ground.

We said our goodbyes to the family and friends, asked for prayer, packed our cases and were ready for off. Like most housewives, I have certain kitchen knives and a pair of scissors I always take with me when we are self-catering. I packed them in my case, but Hugh felt that it would be better if we carried them with our hand luggage. We had had the disruption of unpacking an electric shaver on a previous occasion, so I unpacked the case and put them in my small holdall. Mistake number one! Little did we know how much trouble this would cause us later.

When we got to the security check out in England, obviously my knives and scissors showed up in my hand luggage on the x-ray unit. Calling us to one side an official explained that such articles should have been packed in our suitcase! To me, they were just kitchen utensils, but now, looking at them from a terrorist point of view, they were lethal! The officer told me to collect them when we landed at Tunis. On landing, we took some time finding the Tunisian Security Officer, who handed me my lethal parcel, but by this time, passport control was closed, as all the other passengers had passed through. We waited by the booth for sometime, but no one came to our assistance. Having been though continental controls without having our passports stamped, we came to the conclusion that the same must apply for Tunis, - but were a little puzzled. Just standing at an empty booth seemed ridiculous, we could see an American couple waiting for us, and so, quite innocently, we did not get our passports stamped. Mistake number two!

This was our first meeting with a delightful American family. Bill worked at the US Embassy and Joyce, although at home, became involved with many activities at a local level, and also hosted a weekday ladies' Bible study. We dropped her off to collect the family from school and Bill took us on to Church House. My first impressions are not easy to describe. The door to the house opened straight on to the street, it had at least four locks, and was desperately in need of paint. The street itself was noisy, dirty, and narrow, with many potholes in both road and path. People everywhere seemed to be in a hurry, and laden with all sorts of shopping and using a language I did not understand. I was experiencing my first culture shock, and this was to be my home for the next six weeks!

Bill opened the two locks that worked and we went in; once the door was shut, we were in a different world. The noise was shut out and we walked up some marble steps to a magnificent hall, with marble flooring and wide stairs leading to the floor above. We went into the kitchen first. I noticed a big gas-stove, there was a 'fridge, a freezer and a new looking washing machine, the floor was marble and concrete and the walls very high. The back door, leading into a yard, had iron bars, as did the windows. The tops of the cupboards reached the ceiling, much too high to be practical, but there were ample storage space lower down and shelves with more than enough saucepans for our use. A big kitchen table along one wall with a plastic cloth plus chairs completed the kitchen. As Bill took us over the house it was evident that in the good old days, the chaplains had had many servants, and probably entertained on a large scale. I never counted the number of bedrooms with iron beds and wooden shutters. We later discovered that the best policy in the unused rooms was to leave the shutters as we found them, they were so old and would fall apart if we tried to open them.

All I have described would have been heaven to missionaries one hundred years ago. We had running water, something to cook with, a 'fridge and a washing machine, what more did we need! Going upstairs, a door off the landing led into a small, comfortable sitting room with another door into a bedroom, with bathroom and shower room adjoining. On the bed was a note from Mandy, Bill's younger daughter, welcoming us to Church House and Tunis. That note did me a power of good. Bill took us over to the Church, a substantial stone building, and we talked about services and activities, then he said, "Would you like to pray?" We said yes, and together we committed the time of our chaplaincy into the Lord's hands, knowing that all would be well.

The location of St George's Church and house was in a typically Tunisian setting. Across the road from the Church was a market selling fruit and vegetables and with rows of trestle tables piled high with second-hand clothing. We found a way into one of the many Souks, and walked along the narrow noisy street. The road eventually widened out, and there in front of us, much to our surprise, was the British Embassy. The walk from Church House had taken about twenty minutes.

Near the house we discovered more markets and a bakery, selling the most delicious home made bread, baked daily on the premises and very reasonably priced. We mentioned this to someone who had lived in Tunis for some time and were told that bread carried a government subsidy. When talk of removing this subsidy became public knowledge, there were bread riots!

The first night of our stay we were woken up, while it was still dark, by the call to prayer. This sounded strange, and at first, a bit frightening and uncanny, but we soon got used to it and slept through.

The following morning we went on a tour of inspection of Church House. Outside our bedroom and sitting room windows was a flat roofed area, with washing lines going from one end to the other, a perfect spot for drying. There were also chairs and a table so that one could get quite comfortable sitting outside, but there was always the noise of Tunisian music from a shop selling tapes just across the road. Fortunately in the house it was cool and quiet.

We enjoyed the fresh fruit and vegetables, very reasonably priced, but I always washed them as soon as we got home. Near us was a grocery shop where only Arabic was spoken. When he got to know us the shopkeeper let me go behind the counter to select my own goods if sign language had failed to convey my meaning! We bought all our bottled water and milk from him, and if we had a carton of a dozen or so bottles, he would put them on a trolley and deliver our goods to the door of Church House - he was very helpful. That applied to most of the Tunisians we met; we were sorry we could not speak with them and only use sign language, but even so, we managed to understand each other quite well.

119

A Sunday at St George's began with nine o-clock Bible class for everyone, parents and children alike in their separate groups. The Church House dining room, lounge, and study were all utilised for this, plus a large garden-room for the youngest group. Then over to the Church for a ten o-clock service. Back to the house afterwards for coffee and some form of sweetmeat, cakes or biscuits, with the opportunity for children to play and parents to talk. At six o-clock we met in various homes for Bible study and prayer, while the children played, then got back together again for refreshments, more chat and eventually home. More than once we went to the delightful home of another couple from the States, Brad and Fawn, who were expecting an addition to their already large family! Sunday was an important family day, for worship and pleasure, and they made the most of it. Among the friends we met in this way were folk from both Sweden and Holland, but sadly no British families were present. We did, however, have great pleasure in meeting Sheila from England and enjoyed a visit to Carthage with her, and also Ken, who was teaching English in Tunisia, and helped us in many ways, especially in matters to do with Church house.

While out shopping, we noticed people leading sheep on leads; the market across the road had pens of sheep, in fact as the days went by, we saw sheep everywhere. One evening walking along the street near Church House, we heard a bleating. Looking up we saw a sheep with its head stuck through the balcony railings and making quite a noise, it must have been very frightened. We asked our Church friends what was happening, and were told that on a certain day, the sheep would be killed and eaten, as a thanksgiving for the time when Abraham was willing to offer his son Ishmael (rather than Isaac!) to God and the angel stopped him. Every family had a sheep. The later they left the buying of the sheep, the more expensive they became. A young boy was walking along with a sheep on a lead, we would see him pulling, but the animal seemed to have a mind of it's own and struggled and pulled. Eventually the boy, helped by his friends, won the day and the sheep walked along quietly. More than once we saw men carrying sheep in their arms! Every family had become sheep orientated, some families must have made real sacrifices to buy their sheep. They obviously believed in this ritual, and carried it out faithfully.

Bill and Joyce asked us if we would like to go with the family to Tabarka, a lovely spot along the coast where they would be staying at a very new hotel. We were delighted, especially as it was at the time when the sheep were to be killed! We had a relaxing break and enjoyed the food. Mandy and Lauren swam in the pool, while we relaxed on the loungers. At night we played games. "Uno" was a great favourite. The hotel was near the beach, and walking along the sand we saw small pieces of coral and got quite a collection. The sun shone and the sky was blue, we had good company. This was Tunisia giving us of its best, a beautiful country, and we enjoyed it to the full.

A letter came through the post asking a previous chaplain to report at the police station. Talking this over with Brad and Bill, it was decided we should go to the police and tell them the chaplain had now left Tunis, and that Hugh was acting as chaplain, on a temporary basis, for six weeks but they said, "Do take your passports." We went on the appointed day and waited around before finally getting to the policeman in charge. His English was as good as our Arabic - nil! We showed him our passports on request and he nearly exploded. Our last stamp was from Israel - and there was no entry stamp for Tunisia. He got someone who knew a few words of English, who asked us, mostly in sign language, "How did you get into Tunisia without having your passport stamped?" Trying to explain without a common language was not easy. No one was allowed into Tunis without their passports being stamped, and our last stamp was Israel! We were made fully aware of our problems. At last he made us understand we were to come back, with our passports, and gave us a day and time to report. He also made us understand they would have someone available who could speak English.

We reported to the police station on the right day. There was more waiting about, but eventually we went into a room with two men, one of whom could speak reasonable English. He questioned us both about our visit to Israel and why we had no Tunisian stamp of entry. We could only tell the truth, but the problem for the police was, how had we got into Tunis without having our passports stamped, and what had we been doing in Israel. We were told we must report to a Government Department a few days later.

Getting back to Church House we prayed about the whole matter, and, talking things over with Bill and Brad, were advised to contact the British Consul. The staff were very helpful and said they would send someone with us to the Department who could speak Arabic. Getting to the Embassy in good time we were introduced to the Tunisian man who would accompany us. After a long walk, we found ourselves in a big building, guarded by police with guns, not an easy place to visit, but our friend from the Embassy was a great help. After waiting in a room with many people, where it was hot and stuffy and the seats uncomfortable, we were called into a corridor and told our story to a man who spoke a little English. He asked for our passports and took them away saying, "You must go back and wait." We sat down again in the waiting room. Then our friend from the Embassy was called. He was gone quite a time and came back saying, " I will speak to you outside." We asked, "Have you got our passports?" He answered, "Yes, but you must report with them at eight o'clock tomorrow morning." So back to the Embassy we went, grateful for the help of our friend but anxious to get the matter settled. Talking things over with the Consul, it was decided we should leave our passports in the Embassy safe overnight, and our friend would go to the Department for us the next morning. The Consul asked us to call at ten to have coffee and say goodbye. This was late Thursday afternoon, the Department closed on Friday, and our plane home was booked for Monday afternoon!

A friend rang from Hailsham and we asked for prayer about the passport situation. She rang the Vicar and told him of our plight. So on the Sunday the congregation prayed for us. I think some of them imagined we were in a "Terry Waite" situation! We went to the Embassy on the Friday morning and had coffee with the Consul, he was sure all would be well, and our passports would be returned. We waited and waited. Various members of the staff checked up on us, but still we waited. The Embassy closed at lunchtime on Fridays. By twelve o'clock our concern was great, we had prayed, but felt very much alone, in a strange country, without our passports. We could see out into the area in front of the Embassy from a window and kept looking for our friend. Then, at about 12.30 pm, we saw him walking quickly into the Embassy enclosure, and when he saw us he waved the passports aloft. Our relief was so great; he was so pleased to give us back the precious documents, properly stamped with the date on which we had entered Tunis!

About ten days before we left we had a letter from the Archdeacon of Egypt, asking for accommodation and were happy to oblige. He wanted a bed early in the week, would be taking a flight on to Algeria the next day, and would arrive back on Saturday afternoon to spend the weekend with us, and then get his flight back to Egypt on the Tuesday. Our flight home was for the Monday, before he left. I had discovered he liked homemade jam, and plum jam was one of his favourites. While doing the weekend shopping I noticed a glut of delicious plums, I bought some and made plum jam for him to take home. During our stay I had used the fruit in season to make jam, the latest being apricot. It was delicious, and the Archdeacon appreciated the homemade taste. As I went through the cupboards on the Sunday evening before our departure, I noticed some Andrew's Liver Salts and offered them to him, much to his delight. So much we take for granted in England is unobtainable in Tunis; they do not have our superstores. We found meat a problem. Joyce took us to butchers where meat was kept under refrigeration. This was quite a journey from Church House, and so we got a reasonable amount while we were there as the kitchen had a good freezer. We discovered butchers next door to Church House, the meat was hanging up in the shop, without glass windows, and no protection from dirt and flies. Live chickens were on sale at the market, but we did not fancy dealing with them. I think live fish was available too, but it was easy to fill up with fruit and vegetables and a meagre helping of meat, and I did buy tinned cheese from the market! But always one can adjust, and the "roast beef and Yorkshire pudding" would be something to look forward to once we were home!

With our passports duly stamped, we were ready to leave the many friends made during this unusual chaplaincy. Lauren asked if I would write to her and we are still in touch. Our last service was a Communion taken by the Archdeacon with Hugh preaching. We both felt sadness at leaving such wonderful people; our Christian love and fellowship was a strong and living bond. At the end of the service we were given a book about the history of Tunis, as a farewell gift and a reminder of our visit. We both thanked God for the privilege of serving Him at St George's, Tunis.

The Archdeacon had asked if he could take us out for an evening meal, to repay us for our hospitality, and we were happy to accept. We walked to a restaurant he knew about, but as it was shut he found another; it was busy, but he thought it looked a good place. We had an excellent meal, and for a sweet I chose my favourite, lemon sorbet. It was delicious, but I had forgotten about the water! We had only drunk bottled water the whole of our stay in Tunis, even cleaning our teeth with bottled water. This was the only time I made such a mistake, but it was to prove costly.

Bill and Joyce saw us off. We thought that if anything went wrong Bill could speak up for us, in Arabic. There was no trouble with our passports, we just walked through. As we waved goodbye to Bill and Joyce, we wondered when we would see them again. They had become such special friends. Our daughter Ruth met us at Gatwick and took us to her home in Reigate where we had a meal and saw her family. Then back home to Hailsham and church friends, especially Monica, a former China Inland Mission worker at the Cheefoo school, who had kept an eye on our house and garden in our absence; and Lucy, a near neighbour much given to hospitality, who invited us to lunch the next day.

A memorable visit to the Holy Land 1989

Ruby Wedding Anniversary 1990

As much as we had enjoyed our chaplaincy in Tunis, it was, as always, good to be home. We caught up with the local news of church and friends, admired the garden, sorted out the cases and did a pile of washing, got the shopping organised and enjoyed phone calls from Martin and Paul. Everyone said we were looking well after our working holiday.

As soon as possible we arranged a family get-together with Mark and Ruth, Rachel, Clare and Jonny at Reigate. Martin and Alison, with Vicki, David and Amie would make the journey from Wimborne in Dorset. Paul and Anna were not able to get over from Switzerland.

On the journey to Reigate I suddenly had bad stomach pains, but did not tell Hugh or Monica, who was with us to enjoy the family fun. I felt very "off", but decided to keep quiet and ignore it. I had no desire to spoil the day, and was so much looking forward to seeing everyone again. As I have said, I looked well, and as we talked and caught up with the family news and with the distribution of presents from Tunis, it seemed I was getting away with my plan of silence. But the need to pop upstairs more than once, made me realise there was a problem, so I asked Ruth if she had anything for an upset tummy and took a dose of her remedy.

Lunch was a salad with cold meat. I could not face the salad, but managed a few potatoes and some meat. I have no recollection of our second course, but must have eaten a small portion, and thought I had got away with it.

We had a perfect day. The children are good friends and enjoy each other's company. They climbed the old apple tree, had a go on the swing and climbed the ropes, got the bikes out and played some games. The rest of us just sat around and chatted, a normal family occasion.

We got home about 9 o'clock and I told Hugh my problem. He said, "Why didn't you tell me before?" I said, "It'll probably be all right in the morning, I didn't want to spoil your day." But the next morning it was not all right.

Martin rang to ask if anything was wrong, Alison had noticed I had not eaten much on Saturday and wondered if all was well. We explained the situation and said that if it did not clear up, I would go to doctor.

I saw our doctor, and had tests, but nothing showed up, although the situation was still the same. It was suggested the Hospital for Tropical Diseases might be a good idea. Tiredness was a daily problem and because I was not eating I was losing weight, but after a few visits to the hospital there was an improvement and the Doctor gave me the "all clear" from the bug I had picked up.

I still felt unwell, however, and noticed that even walking upstairs made me breathless now, and as the tiredness never left me, everything was an effort. When I made an appointment to see my own doctor again and explained the symptoms, he was very understanding. After examining me, he said, "I want you to have some chest X-rays." On the right day, and the right time, I presented myself at the X-ray Department of our local district hospital and joined the queue! By this time, just speaking normally was a problem, I needed to stop for breath, and pause, even in the middle of a sentence, which was not a bit like me.

As is usual with X-rays, I was asked to wait until the radiologist was satisfied with the result, but everyone was getting permission to dress, but me. A young man in a white coat came along asking for Mrs Hulbert. I got up from my chair, puffing a bit, and walked towards him. He said, "I'm so sorry to have kept you waiting, but the X-rays show fluid on your lung. I have just rung your doctor. He will get in touch with you."

I found Hugh in the waiting room and told him the result. He was aghast. We were both shaken by the fact that it was being taken so seriously, although we knew I was far from well. Feeling a cup of tea would be a good idea, we went to the excellent WRVS food bar, still wondering just what had hit us.

A dear friend from church, Gladys, had been in hospital for some time and as we sat drinking our tea we said it would be a good idea to visit her. As in all hospitals, whatever your destination, it's a long way off! We completed the journey to her ward, but I made the mistake of thinking I could walk up the stairs, and could hardly get my breath before we were half way up. This was nasty! The sooner it was cleared up, the better, as far as we were concerned.

Gladys was so pleased to see us, but we did not stay long, just long enough to chat, have some prayer, and say how much we loved and missed her.

We arrived home, to be told by Alan, a friend, who was doing some decorating for us, that our doctor had telephoned, and would ring again later. We were not surprised when he rang and said, "I have made an appointment for you to see a chest consultant as soon as possible." This was proving to be quite a day!

We rang Martin, Paul and Ruth, and one or two other friends, to tell them our news and ask for their prayer.

I saw the consultant a few weeks later, who wanted me to go into hospital for tests and the removal of fluid from my lung. Until the tests were made, he could not say precisely what was wrong with me.

On the Friday evening before I was due to go into hospital, I started to feel very ill, and my temperature shot up. Hugh rang the surgery. Our own GP was not on duty, but his colleague came, and after examining me, said, "I want you in hospital over the weekend." This was unexpected, I said, "I'm due to see the chest consultant on Tuesday, could I wait until then?" but he said, "No, you must go into hospital tonight, I don't want you at home over the weekend. I'll ring for an ambulance." He assured me it was for my own good, and by this time, I was ready to agree with him.

While we were waiting for the ambulance, Hugh held my hands and prayed. I was so moved when I heard him say, "Please Lord, may Grace be near someone with whom she can have Christian fellowship."

We arrived at the hospital after nine o'clock and by the time my case history was completed it was well after ten o'clock, and Hugh left.

I was in an admissions ward, and looking around me, realised it was a six bedded ward, consisting of five men and myself, and I had an illness not yet diagnosed. I was afraid, lonely and anxious. Then the thought came to me:'I am going to spend the night with five strange men!'

I asked, "What about Hugh's prayer, Lord?"

The following morning, I was pushed in my bed, along corridors, and steered in to Gladys's ward. There by her bed was an empty space, just for me! I was given oxygen, which proved a great help.

We had a time of gentle Christian love and fellowship and got to know each other even better. Not many weeks afterwards Gladys went to be with her Lord. We thanked God for the way He had answered Hugh's prayer. He knew that Gladys needed my love and fellowship, just as much as I needed hers. Gladys went home on Monday, my treatment started on Tuesday.

On Tuesday fluid was removed from my lung, and a biopsy was taken. Afterwards I was very tired and went into an exhausted sleep and woke up to see something red on a stool at the side of the bed. Opening my eyes wider I saw Pauline, our vicar's wife, sitting on a stool. She was wearing a red blouse and smiled at me saying, "Hello." That visit was really important. To see someone I knew, at such a time, was a great comfort. Plus the fact that she was wearing my favourite colour! Pauline works in the laboratory at the hospital and had popped up to see me during a quiet spell.

Having fluid drained from my lung made a difference, but they would not take any more off in case my lung collapsed. The consultant thought I could have tuberculosis, and said it was easily cleared up by tablets, but he could not be sure until he had the results of the tests.

After treatment and a rest, I went home. I had an appointment to see the consultant a few days later. I was still short of breath, finding it difficult to finish a sentence without pausing for breath, and was using a Red Cross wheelchair by this time.

My next appointment was for 4.30 pm on a dark evening, early in January. We were so thankful Monica came along with us, to get me organised, while Hugh parked the car.

We were the only ones waiting to see the consultant when the nurse called me. I got out of the wheelchair and walked with Hugh into the consulting room, feeling weak and wobbly. After greeting us and getting us seated, the doctor looked up from his notes and said, very quietly, looking me full in the face, "Mrs Hulbert, I am sorry to have to tell you that you have not got tuberculosis. The tests show that you have an inoperable tumour on your left lung."

My whole being cried out, "Not again, Lord!"

I looked at Hugh. He reached out and put his hand over mine. We had just hit rock bottom with a mighty bang. Knowing the result of such a prognosis, I realised how much I loved him. The thought of leaving him was awful. Then I thought of my wonderful family: Martin, Paul and Ruth, Alison, Anna and Mark, Vicki, David, Amie, Rachel, Clare and Jonny. I would never see the children grow up. One's thoughts at such a time are all jumbled up, and yet very clear. I realised then the depth of my love for my family and friends, and in some strange way I thought, "This love is God given and so precious. Thank you, Lord."

The consultant prescribed morphine, Tamoxofen and steroids, because I could not eat and was losing weight. He made an appointment for me to go into hospital and have more fluid withdrawn.

Hugh went outside while he did more tests. As I was leaving the consulting room, with my hand on the door handle, I turned and looked at the doctor, busy writing at his desk (rather like Douglas, the desk I had bought for Hugh over 40 years ago), and knew he was a man I could trust. I said, "Thank you for being honest with me. I know I can trust you, and for someone in my place, that is essential." This thought was a great comfort to me.

I got home exhausted and went to bed. Monica was staying with us by this time, as I needed day and night attention. I was waking up in a profuse sweat, and had to change my nightie and sheets before I could get comfortable again. Most of my days were spent in bed. If I got downstairs for "Countdown", I was pleased. Every afternoon just before 4.30 pm our very dear friend, Lucy, would come in to watch it with us and have a cup of tea, or come upstairs and chat, if I was still in bed, while Monica and Hugh sat down for half an hour. I was living in a "No go" area, and only just holding on! Lucy is one of the most practical people I have ever met. Without interfering, she always helps her friends and acquaintances wherever she can. She did all our ironing, and still does! One is rich with such friends. Monica and Lucy make a good pair; we are greatly blessed and thank God for them.

For some years now, Hugh and I have read the Bible through in a year, starting in January and finishing in December. We find it is easier to make the time in retirement, and I did not want to let this go. Time was not my problem, but dropping off to sleep was! I remembered a "Living Bible" on the bookshelves, and asked Hugh to bring it up for me next time he came. I had not read it for some years, and on opening it, found a green leather bookmark with Philippians 4: 6,7 written in gold with a praying hands motif at the top. I read the words:

"Have no anxiety about anything, but in everything by prayer and supplication with thanksgiving, let your requests be made known to God. And the peace of God which passes all understanding, will keep your hearts and minds in Christ Jesus."

The thought came to me: "This should be my daily prayer." From that time on, whenever I read my Bible, those verses became my prayer of thanksgiving and expectancy. Anything that made me anxious or worried was turned into prayer by those words. I was getting "back to basics", and even in my situation began to experience that "Peace of God which passes

132

all understanding." It was certainly beyond my understanding, but it was happening to me, and I just thanked and praised my, "Prince of Peace" for keeping my heart and mind in His peace.

From the onset of my illness I had set my mind to read God's word and to pray, while this was possible, and my body allowed me to do so. I have had people say to me, "I cannot cope with Bible reading when I'm ill." I fully understand that, but my own experience tells me you have to set your mind to read and pray and not be deterred, just go on, no matter what, until this is no longer possible. As we meditate on the word of God and let it "dwell in us richly", the Holy Spirit has His own way of bringing texts to our hearts and our minds, and making them stand out in such bold print, we cannot ignore them. They are in your body, your mind and your spirit, a wonderful gift of the Spirit from our ever loving Heavenly Father. In case this sounds rather cosy and over pious, and not a bit like me, perhaps the following incident will explain what I mean.

One morning I started reading Ephesians and was struck by verse 4 of the first chapter, especially the last part of the verse which reads: "We who stand before Him covered with His love." The thought went round and round in my head and was printed on my heart: "When I stand before God, I will be covered with His love, because of Jesus. My sins are covered, cleansed, thrown into the depths of the sea, Jesus loves me and died for me on Calvary, I am free, the truth had made me 'free indeed'."

That was not a good day and I stayed in bed, sometimes dropping off to sleep, but waking up unrefreshed. Late in the afternoon I woke from a fitful sleep and the thought came very strongly: "You are dying." I had a tightening up all over my body and felt very much afraid. Fear had me in its grip; I can only describe it as a dark, unending, overwhelming fear, completely devoid of love. Spontaneously the words, "We stand before Him covered with His love" came into my mind and God's love flowed through me, and the fear vanished.

The power of God's word in 1 John 4:18 became a living reality within me. "There is no fear in love. But perfect love drives out fear, because fear has to do with punishment. The one who fears is not made perfect in love." Love, joy and peace seemed to flow like waves over me and through me and fill me with God's love. I knew then, with absolute clarity, that nothing would stop me seeing my "Mighty God and Everlasting Father," my "Wonderful Counsellor and Prince of Peace," except sin!

God would not say to me when I saw him, "You've worked for me many years on earth and deserve a rest, come in." No, I knew with every part of my being, the only way to be with Him forever was to be "clothed with His love" and therefore sinless. I prayed: "Father, cleanse me from any sin I have committed, if I know of it or not", and then said, "Thank you, I know the blood of Jesus Christ your son, cleanses me from all sin." To die was simply to go to Him forever and leave this weary body. To die was to see His face and, as He saw me in Jesus, to hear Him say, "Well done, good and faithful servant." That was life, not death, real life, eternal life! As His child, eternal life had been my gift when I gave my life to Him in 1945, and I was ready to claim it. Words cannot explain my feelings except to say overwhelming love, joy, peace, freedom, happiness and security flooded my body, mind and spirit. Every part of me was experiencing "the peace of God which passes all understanding". As 1 Peter 1:8 puts it: "Though you have not seen him, you love him, and even though you do not see him now, you believe in him and are filled with an inexpressible and glorious joy." I will never forget what God did for me that day.

Filled with a new energy, that was almost too much for me to handle, I remember saying, "Don't forget I'm ill, Father, I'm finding all this very tiring to cope with."

As I lay there, I thought of God's word to Monica one Sunday morning, while I was still getting over my tummy troubles. She was in church with Hugh, listening to the choir singing the "Jubilate Deo" as an anthem, when she heard a voice say quite clearly, "Grace is going to get well." We thought at the time it meant my tummy, but I know now, it was the tumour.

If I was to believe God had spoken to Monica, there must be no doubt in my mind. Asking her about it I said, "Please don't tell me what you want, just tell me what you heard, if you really heard it." I was still unsure. She answered, "If I said I did not hear a voice, I would be telling a lie." That convinced me. From then on I believed her, and would say to myself over and over again that God had said, "Grace is going to get well." I was going to get well, because God had said so; whatever way round, it was the same thing and now I believed it too!

There was no change in my condition, I was just hanging on, but wonderfully supported by the love of my family and friends. Letters and cards were such a comfort, flowers and small gifts made their way to the front door. Until then, I had no idea so many people were praying for us as a family, and I was able to rest in their love and care. To show love, concern and care to a friend who is unwell and going through a difficult time is a wonderful help. To say "We love you and are praying for you" is a great source of comfort and strength, but only if it is true. I learnt a valuable lesson on my sick bed, simply this, that when I love someone in Jesus, friend or family, I say so, and try to put actions to words. No one knows the number of their days, that one time may be the only opportunity you will ever get to say, "I love you." Don't miss it!

My cards from the grandchildren were a great delight. A big brown envelope with a Dorset or Reigate postmark usually meant get-well cards, in their own individual style. Some stand out in my mind.

One from David said, "Dear Granny, Get well soon. Here is a sum for you to do." David never wasted words when writing, but he enjoyed sums, and was sending me the best thing he could, namely, a sum to do.

Amie sent a card saying, "Dear granny, GET WELL SOON, can you see that?" The "GET WELL SOON" was in big capital letters. She was making quite sure I got the message.

While I was still coping with the tummy problems, a card from Vicki with an intricate pattern around the words "Don't get well soon" puzzled visitors to my kitchen, and when they

135

saw it stuck on the fridge door they asked, "What does it mean?" I said, "Open the card and see." Inside were the words, "Get well now!"

Rachel and Clare pressed some autumn leaves in beautiful reds, browns and tans. Rachel made a leaf and flower pattern; it was so lovely and hung in a plain glass frame in my kitchen until we moved.

Clare made a leaf picture. I enjoyed looking at it, so I got another frame to show its beauty, and hung that too in the kitchen. My grandchildren were certainly showing talent and they knew I was interested in the things they made for me.

One of Jonny's cards was of a house, with a door and windows that opened. Across the top were the words, "Stay in Jesus." He was about six at the time and I thought, "That is profound, how on earth can a six year old send such a message?" I asked his mother Ruth about it and she said, "Ask Jonny." I did and his reply was, "Well - we were doing a spelling test at school and had to spell the word 'stay'. I thought it was a nice word, so I gave it to you." I had never been given a nice word before and enjoyed the experience!

Lauren, the young American girl we met in Tunisia sent letters and cards, one card said, "We must have courage, faith and lunch together sometime soon!" Hugh still has it on the filing cabinet by his desk, I can see it as I sit at the computer. Another card from Lauren said, "Miracles happen to those who believe in them." I put the card near the kitchen sink and any time I was in the kitchen, I would read it and say to myself, "That's what I believe, thank you Lord." Writing this makes me realise how positive my thoughts and beliefs were, but in no way was I practising auto-suggestion.

These things were wonderful, but I was still very ill. I did believe the words Monica had heard, "Grace is going to get well", and they were a great comfort, but I made no real improvement.

One morning the thought came into my mind, "I could ask God to heal me now." I prayed a simple prayer, "Heal me now,

Father, I know you can", but nothing happened. I was still the same the following morning. I felt rather down, and lost the peace of mind that had been my daily experience. As the day wore on, the feeling of despair grew. I knew God was not answering my prayer and I began to magnify my symptoms. I had been trusting in the words, "Have no anxiety about anything ..." But my peace had gone; I was worried to bits. What was wrong with me? Surely as I was so ill, God would answer me?

Knowing something was wrong, I asked God for help ... not healing. I kept quiet, just meditating and listening, not saying anything. As I was still, the Holy Spirit showed me that I had lost my belief in the words, "Grace is going to get well", wanting Him to go my way, not His. My desire had been to get well now, at this moment, not leave the whole thing in His hands. I asked for forgiveness and said, "I am sorry, I know I have sinned, albeit with the best of intentions, now all I want to do is to go your way, not mine."

How subtle the devil is, how he manipulates our thoughts and minds, especially when we are ill. This is his work, and he always hits us hardest when we are down. As an angel of light, he said to me, "Ask God to make you well now." In other words, "You know better than God. As you are so ill, ask Him to make you well now, He is bound to do as you ask because He loves you. All this waiting to get well is taking far too long."

How we need God's word in our hearts and minds, so that we can answer the devil with the sword of the spirit. Just as Jesus did.

But we must tell our Heavenly Father just how we feel, it's not wrong. Just pour it all out (but don't whine at Him). He knows our heartache and pain. He cares about us. He has written our name on the palm of His hand, He will never leave us or forsake us. We are loved with an everlasting love.

The Psalms were such a help as I read, "Be merciful to me, Lord, for I am faint; O Lord, heal me, for my bones are in agony. My soul is in anguish. How long, O Lord, how long? Turn O Lord, and deliver me; save me because of your unfailing love ... My heart is in anguish within me; the terrors of death assail me. Fear and trembling have beset me; horror has overwhelmed me. I said, "Oh, that I had the wings of a dove! I would fly and be at rest." Psalms 6:2-4, and 55:4-6.

I did not make great strides. After going into hospital for the first fluid draining, I was a little better, but knew there was need for more treatment. Part of this treatment was to have my lung stuck together, to contain the tumour, but the first time it did not work! The next time was successful, although I am not aware of any difference in my body. I had two more sessions, more X-rays and saw the consultant again. He said, "You still have a lot of gunge down there, I'm going to try you on another method of draining. We will put a tube in your lung with a bag attached to the end, but it must never come higher than your waistline, whatever you are doing, awake or asleep." And that was how I got my personal "doggy bag" on the National Health Service. While I was in bed, Hugh attached it to our upright Hoover, otherwise it hung around my neck and came with me wherever I went. Without a sense of humour, we would not have coped. Rachel, Clare and Jonny saw me at this stage and, at first, were not too sure of the doggy bag, but got used to it after a short time.

I was now beginning to sit up and take notice. Walking or standing was still a problem. I was breathing more easily and not needing oxygen. A great step forward, but I could do very little for myself.

Our doctor had said he wanted me to have an Attendance Allowance at the onset of my illness and brought me the necessary forms to fill in. There were two types, one for general disability, the other for "People with a terminal illness, not expected to live more than 6 months." I got the latter. It was a help, because of necessity, we were living a much more expensive lifestyle. More heating, I was always cold, unless I was sweating, there was no happy medium. Loads more washing and more frozen foods. Sometimes a taxi to the hospital, and help in the house, to name but a few things. Hugh put his back out, getting the wheelchair in and out of the car when I was in the middle of treatment. We were asked not to use the ambulance unless absolutely necessary, but it was much quicker by taxi. The taxi drivers were wonderful, very understanding and helpful, especially when they saw the doggy bag, and got the wheelchair in and out of the car with no difficulty. This was six months after my diagnosis. At least I was still alive!

Having breakfast in bed one morning and looking across the green to the bungalows in Milland Road, I said, "Lord, I wish we lived in a bungalow." This was just between God and myself, not even Hugh, but the thought of no stairs was like heaven to me. I was beginning to have very short walks, my first was to Lucy, just across the green, and she made me a very welcome cup of tea. As the days went by we planned short walks, ending at a seat, where I would have a rest, and then make my way home. Hugh took me out one day, and when we reached the seat and sat down, he looked at me very seriously and said, "I wish we lived in a bungalow." I could not believe my ears as I asked, "Do you have a bungalow in mind?" "Yes," came the answer, "I'll show you on the way home." It was 43 Milland Road.

As far as we knew the bungalow was occupied and as we have an equity mortgage with the Clergy Pensions Board, we thought no more about it. Hugh mentioned our hopes to a friend who lives in Milland Road and said, "If ever a three bedroom bungalow becomes vacant, let us know." I thought that in any case I could never manage a move and left it at that. After all, we did enjoy our house, apart from the stairs, which were a continual problem to me.

About three or four miles out of Hailsham is Glyndley Manor, no longer the home of the lord of the manor, but a conference centre for the healing ministry, part of Ellel Ministries. People come from many parts of the world to attend the courses, some lasting three months, others a week or weekend. Every two months they have an open evening, inviting anyone needing ministry to go forward for prayer, there is no pressure, although anyone with problems is under a certain amount of inward pressure, that is why they are there. One evening we went along and I went forward for prayer, breathless, not able to stand and very tired. It was a big thing, even to get up the stairs to the conference room, although going down was just as bad! Inwardly I believed God had said, "Grace is going to get well", but my body showed little improvement. Ringing Glyndley Manor later, I asked to speak to the person who had talked and prayed with me, and said, "Nothing has happened, can you help me?" The reply was, "Yes," and we arranged a time to meet.

I received the most loving and caring counselling and truly thank God for the impact this made on my life. I realised my life was like an iceberg, so much of me, the inner me, was submerged, and needed to be brought to the surface and dealt with, in the name of Jesus. But only by those who knew what they were doing. I met my two counsellors many times. Their counselling was new to me, but I went along with them and knew, as we dealt with past difficulties in my life, there was a need to be free in the Name of Jesus from memories that were holding me down in grief. Some I did not even realise were there: even memories in my parents' and grandparents' lives. I was asked about my parents, and as I said, "My father died of lung cancer", the full impact of this came home to me, and I realised afresh the significance of the blood of Jesus to cleanse me, and the broken body of Jesus to carry my griefs and sorrows.

There is no fear in such counselling, just complete freedom, as Jesus takes away the pain of the past. As we talked about my father, I mentioned that he was reported missing, believed killed in the battle of the Somme. When the fighting was over, some nuns went around the battlefields looking for soldiers still alive, but wounded. My father must have groaned as they approached him - he was still alive. They found a jacket or coat nearby and wrapped him in it and sent him to the field hospital, where he was quickly sent back to England. As the

140

jacket had papers belonging to a northern regiment in a pocket, he was sent up north, and my grandparents had a telegram to say their son was missing, believed killed. When my father realised what had happened, things were soon put right. I have always been so grateful to those dedicated nuns. As we talked and prayed about this, I had a strange feeling, as though my body was coming out through wet, soggy, light brown mud. My arms were by my side, and I was covered with mud. One of the counsellors was quoting scripture to me. As she spoke, the words were like a strong jet of water, washing all the mud away and I was clean. Whatever happened that day I will never forget. It was not my imagination, but part of God's healing for me. Jesus took the deep grief and I knew God's comfort.

Along with many young men, my father had responded to the poster saying, "Your country needs you." With my mother's brother, he had gone along to the recruiting office, put his age up, and joined the army. Mother's brother was killed; more grief in the family. In my heart I have always hated that poster, feeling it was patriotic, emotional blackmail. Every time I saw it, my feelings were stirred. Why did the government allow such a poster to be splashed all over the country? So many young men were killed in response to that poster - it was so wrong. My counsellors helped me to realise it was not possible to pray, "Forgive me my sins Lord" if I was not willing to "forgive those who sin against me". Although I knew this, I had a blind spot where the poster was concerned. Quite simply, I said sorry, and asked for forgiveness for those who had promoted the poster. Writing it down now, it seems so silly, but it was not then, and needed to be dealt with in the name of Jesus. I was immediately freed from all the hatred aroused by that poster.

My next appointment at the hospital was encouraging, especially when I told the consultant I no longer needed morphine and had been off it for some weeks, with no ill effects. I was still using Distalgesic, when necessary, and of course, still taking Tamoxafen. He was surprised. He could see I was no longer in a wheelchair.

141

Later, seeing my doctor for a routine check, I asked him, "What has happened to the cancer?" He replied, "It has shrivelled up!"

CHAPTER 13
HOME AGAIN

Hugh and I never cease to wonder at God's ways, they are indeed 'past finding out'. We agreed a bungalow would be even better than our very nice house, but felt it was just a dream. Until, that is, our friend rang to say, "A three bedroom bungalow is going to be put on the market, are you interested? It is 43 Milland Road!"

Hugh rang the Pensions Board, and to his surprise, they were willing to let us investigate the possibilities of a move. He contacted the owners, who told him that the property had not yet been put on the market but they were willing to have us meet them at the bungalow that evening at 8 pm I was not able to go round, but Martin, who was staying the night, went with Hugh and they came back thrilled with all they had seen. Martin said, "I think you would be very happy there, it has a peaceful atmosphere."

The negotiations went ahead, and although there was a delay in selling our house, eventually the sale and purchase were completed. We still praise the Lord for the way He gave us the bungalow. Even now there are times I stop whatever I'm doing and say, "Thank you, Lord." This was nine months after the diagnosis, and I was still getting better, but not able to do much. With a move in view, our friends, especially our house group, came up trumps. We had a young man to assist with some of the heavy jobs. After helping us for a few days Gary asked me, "Do you watch Houseparty? All the time different people come into your house and do various jobs and go, then somebody else comes along to do something else. I've noticed they are all smiling and happy, just as they are in Houseparty." One day Hugh asked Gary if he would take the oxygen cylinder back to the chemist, it was quite heavy. When he returned, Hugh thought he looked rather upset, and asked what was wrong. He said, "The person who took the cylinder said, 'I suppose the lady has died'." This really upset him. When Hugh told me I laughed and said, "But Gary, I'm not dead, I'm still alive and getting better every day." He is such a nice young man, thoughtful and hardworking, but finding it hard to get permanent work.

It was on the 14th October 1993, that we finally moved into 43, Milland Road. Rain was forecast but to our delight kept away from our Southeast corner of the country. Our friends and house group members were wonderful and worked really hard. The first piece of furniture Hugh bought into the bungalow was my reclining deckchair, enabling me to sit and give orders, when necessary. We fell into bed, tired, happy and contented. To live in a bungalow was a dream we never thought possible, but I believe in miracles!

The following summer was very hot. Athough my general health was improving, I still had to rest quite a bit. Sitting on my reclining chair, not the garden chair, I felt the sweat pouring off my body. Turning to Hugh, probably doing Tough Puzzles, I said, "Darling, all I'm doing is sitting on my chair and breathing, and my clothes are wet with sweat." His unexpectedly helpful answer was, "Well my dear, stop breathing!"

As I have become stronger and more mobile the twenty minute walk into town and gentle gardening are some of the things I am beginning to enjoy again, albeit in moderation. God is keeping His promise to me, "Grace is going to get well."

CHAPTER 14
THANK YOU, LORD

Every two months we have a healing service in our church. A quiet, helpful time, with prayer at the communion rail for any in need. I was asked if I would speak for five minutes at the next service, and was told I could remain seated while speaking. I agreed and mentioned this to a friend who said, "Ask Hugh to pray for your protection while you are speaking." I was surprised, but we did as had been suggested. Later, going forward to two friends for prayer, one looked at me and said, "Grace, such a thing has never happened to me before, but I must tell you, while you were speaking, I saw an angel standing behind you. He was very tall, and had a drawn sword in his hand, he was protecting you." No one else had seen a thing! This whole episode of my life is beyond my understanding, but not beyond my faith. I believed God, in His great wisdom and love for me, knew such encouragement was important, just as He made His Word come alive and real to me when I needed it.

Before going for a scan a friend rang and said, "I'm sure God has given you Psalm 138, verse 8, from the Good News Bible today" and read over the telephone, "You will do what you have promised, Lord your love is eternal, complete what you have begun." The scan was clear!

Talking things over with our own doctor, he said it would be a good idea if Hugh and I went to our local Leisure Centre for a workout. He gave us a prescription, we made an appointment and had a thorough medical check before going on any of the apparatus. Six minutes on the treadmill was my limit, about five on the bicycle, and after a few weeks, five minutes on the rower, with lots of rests in between. This was followed by and tea and scones in the cafeteria, to get us on our feet again! We enjoyed our sessions and made friends with others having a workout, like us, under doctor's prescription.

Some time later Stephanie, in charge of this part of the centre, asked us if we would like to be on the "Kilroy-Silk Show", to say what benefit we had received from our workouts. We were delighted to say yes. The great day came, we were collected by car and made the journey to a sports centre in west London, where we met some of the staff from our Hailsham centre and had coffee or tea, delicious titbits and cake. Later we were taken into an area, with seating and lighting, and all the paraphernalia associated with an outside television broadcast.

The show started, and was recorded to be broadcast the next day. We were impressed with Kilroy-Silk; he knew everything and everyone as he moved around with the microphone, asking questions. The subject under discussion was the use of steroids for bodybuilding: was it a good thing or not? How far was one prepared to go to get a perfect body? Did it really make sense to take five years to reach your target by workouts, or was it wiser to take steroids and do it the easy way? A young doctor was against the use of steroids in body building, but a young man, selling steroids - I think from his garage - said, "I am always careful and explain the dosage and sell only the right dose." When asked, "Do you have any medical training?" he said, "No, but I know what I'm talking about!"

Some had gone over the top to get a perfect body, and ended up with a body damaged for life, and tragically one young boy had died. I sat thinking how awful it is to misuse the body that God has given us by taking tablets that could benefit only the people selling them. There was no reference to exercising on prescription, until Brenda, who works at the centre, had her say. She was good and to the point; the young doctor and others agreed with her. The microphone got nearer to me. I wondered what I would say when my turn came? I was asked what I felt about the use of steroids and said, "I've been sitting here listening to your arguments and would like to say that some people don't know how fortunate they are that they can breathe." I explained why I had found breathing so difficult and how the workouts had improved my breathing ability, and my general health. Hugh, when asked a question, said, "I think we should use the body God has given us and not misuse it" and spoke of the benefit he had received from the workouts, and how much we both enjoyed the sessions. Along with Brenda we changed the direction of the programme and got a good reception from those agreeing with us. When filming was finished Kilroy-Silk made his way towards me, tapped my shoulder and said, "Well done." I was surprised and pleased.

My next appointment at the hospital turned out to be a red-letter day. I told the consultant about the workouts and discovered he was in full agreement. I then said, "Can I do any damage to my lung by these workouts, how much 'breathing-ability' have I got?" - I was remembering that my lung had been stuck together. Doctor replied, "In no way can you damage your lung, go ahead with all you are doing." He then said, "I will examine you and get you X-rayed to see what is going on." We came back and gave the X-rays to the nurse. After a little time nurse called me in, as we walked towards the consulting room she was smiling all over her face, and said, "Wonderful news, we are so pleased." The consultant was seated, but on seeing me he got up and shook my hand saying, "Mrs Hulbert, you have seventy-five per cent breathing-ability in your lung, the rest is scar tissue." Looking me straight in the eye he said, "You have done this yourself." I shook his hand saying, "No, doctor, I've had some help, and know that without you I would not be standing here anyway. Thank you." We walked out of the clinic on air, two and a half years after receiving the first diagnosis of an inoperable tumour of the left lung. Our hearts were full of praise and thanksgiving to God.

I am now on a six-monthly check up. I do get tired and usually have an afternoon rest, but I console myself that so do many other people. God said, "Grace is going to get well." and this is still happening. At times I say to myself, "You could not do that three months ago."

Singing has always been a great joy to me, but for about two years I could not pitch a note, let alone sing it, and any high note was impossible. I just stopped and left it to the rest of the congregation, joining in with them as soon as they had got down to my level; but now apart from the psalms I'm singing with everybody else, except the very high notes. This gives me great joy, I've always sung around the house, but as Hugh will tell you, my personal church calendar will not be found in the Prayer Book. "The day thou gavest Lord has ended" really gets me going first thing in the morning. I sing carols any time of the year, whenever one takes my fancy, Harvest and Easter hymns have no time limit when I'm really going, knowing them so well, I just like to sing. "In the bleak midwinter," is just right in a heat wave! But worship songs so often say what I feel: -

"When I feel the touch of your hand upon my life

It causes me to sing a song that I love You, Lord.

So from deep within my spirit singeth unto thee

You are my King, You are my God, and I love You, Lord."

That I can sing any time of the day or night, it's so true, "I love You, Lord."

The years have flown by and it is now January 1996, my problems started in January 1993. Looking back over the past year, three holidays stand out in my mind. Paul, Anna, Oliver and Leona visited us at the end of May for about 2 weeks. I never thought I would see Paul and Anna's first child, let alone their second. Holding Leona for the first time I thought, "God is giving me one blessing after another, thank you Lord for letting me cuddle her." One Saturday all the family got together, 16 of us, Monica made 17; we had a wonderful time, it was a beautiful day, not too hot, we enjoyed the garden, and the boys kicked a ball about. Oliver thought this was great fun, especially when Jessie (Ruth and Mark's dog) joined in.

To save work in the kitchen, we went Chinese. Martin and Paul know more about these foods than we do and set off for our local takeaway. The food was delicious; eating the meal was great fun, using chopsticks! Monica was a missionary with the former China Inland Mission, and still enjoys Chinese food. Martin took a photograph of the family, the first one of us all together, quite an achievement, and Jessie got in on the act. We now have a delightful family photograph, the only fair-haired

148

one among us is Oliver; Hugh has at least got one blonde grandchild!

We had a wonderful holiday on the Island of Mull with Ruth, Mark, Rachel, Clare and Jonny, not forgetting Jessie. The family stayed in a cottage, at the back of beyond, with birds, sheep, deer and the sea for company, right away from it all, an ideal setting. They revelled in it and plan to go back again this year. We stayed in a delightful hotel about two miles away and got together for outings, or just staying in the cottage and exploring the area. We painted shells collected from the beach, I was given some for a Christmas present - a happy reminder of a perfect holiday. We had haggis with potatoes, carrots and peas, delicious. What a pity we cannot buy haggis in Hailsham!

We visited Torosay Castle, a must if you are in that part of the world. It is a family home, but visitors are made so welcome. Notices explain various articles in the room, and one is actually invited to touch. I took advantage of the invitation to, "sit down and rest and enjoy the room." Beautiful bowls of fresh flowers from the gardens made one feel at home, obviously a woman's touch.

In the dining room was a huge sideboard, almost half the width of the room, a magnificent piece of furniture, years of polishing and care showed in the beauty of the wood. Too big, even for our Portsmouth vicarage I thought! Seeing a notice telling us the history of this masterpiece, I read, "When a former owner of Torosay Castle died his wife had to leave the castle. She took all the furniture with her, but the sideboard defeated all efforts of removal, and was the only piece of furniture she had to leave behind." Presumably it was prefabricated and put together inside the dinning room!

One room was given over to the life story of David James, the previous owner. He was in the Navy during the Second World War, and was captured by the Germans, but escaped from the prison camp. The uniform he altered for his escape was in a glass case, with a notice telling us of his exploits. Alongside there were further details of his life, after his escape. Reading down I was impressed, thinking, "What a remarkable man." Then I read, "After a holiday, he went for a health check. It was discovered he had lung cancer. He fought it all the way, never giving up, living life to the full, until the cancer finally won."

Roy Castle came into my mind; his death made a great impact on me and left me feeling empty inside. Roy was a great man, and a remarkable Christian, and showed much courage in his fight against lung cancer, doing all he could to encourage others to do the same. His wife Fiona, in spite of her grief, lives life to the full, caring for the family, and, through the media, becoming involved in Christian work and witness. With a friend, we went to a breakfast where Fiona Castle was the speaker. Afterwards I told Hugh I would like to meet her and joined a queue, waiting for a word. When we met, I could not speak, words would not come, I just stood in front of her, my heart full of understanding and compassion for such a brave lady. Its not often I'm lost for words! Then Hugh came along and helped me out.

I suppose the reason I'm writing this book is to say, "Thank you," to God, and to encourage anyone to look to Jesus, whatever their problem. He alone is the answer. As Christians, we believe that when we die, we shall see Him "face to face." I also know that if illness is making an end to life, there is no need to fear. I'm not saying we will not fear, experience pain, illness or any other adversity, we will, we are only human, but at Calvary Jesus conquered sin and death, He died in our place and offers us eternal life, if we come to Him by way of the cross. His love for us is greater than anything that can ever happen to us. Recently two of our church friends died from cancer, they were wonderful people and I will miss them. I have no answer to the question, "Why the pain and the parting?" but I know I will see them again. Death has lost its sting because, "The sting of death is sin, but thanks be to God who gives us the victory through our Lord Jesus Christ."

I am thinking of Ann from Worthing as I write this, in the name of Jesus, God took the sting of death away from her, and filled her with his love, and I would dare to add, His joy and His peace.

150

I have diverged a bit from Torosay Castle, but meeting Jacquitta James, David's widow, in the garden there was such an encouragement. Although the Castle was entailed to their son, she still lives there, and one feels her gracious influence on the home they both loved.

As we talked about David, she mentioned a poem. She had forgotten most of it and where she first read it, but even the fragment that she remembered sums up much of what I feel:

"Cancer kills, but so do cars and sleeping pills ... Don't humour your tumour ..."

If anyone knows the verses and could send them to me, I would be so grateful. Such a poem should have pride of place in every Cancer Clinic.

Later in our holiday we dropped down to the Welsh coast to join Martin and Alison with Vicki, David and Amie. They camped; we found bed and breakfast nearby, with an evening meal if we wanted it. The beaches were perfect for surfing, the family all swim and enjoy a day on the beach. I was finishing "The Moonstone" by Wilkie Collins, and paddled, waving to Vicki in the canoe, or just sat and watched the world go by. I remember thinking, as I watched the family, "This is a bonus, every day is a bonus, something to thank God for." Hugh got on with, "Tough Puzzles." Along with other children, David and Amie collected large pebbles, and tried to keep the incoming tide at bay. They worked hard, with our help, but as usual, the tide won, as King Canute could have told them. We were just doing the ordinary everyday things that families get involved with on the beach year after year, but it was special, again, something to thank God for, but then life especially during the last three years, has taught me to say, with all my being, "Thank you God, for everything."

Early in January I went for a check up, the consultant I had known from the start of my illness had retired, another doctor was standing in for a week, his face was one big smile, as he said "How are you feeling Mrs Hulbert?" I replied, "Fine, I do get tired, and a bit breathless at times, but I feel well and am so thankful for all that has been done for me." Referring to my notes he read out the result of a previous blood check, medically it was beyond me. He said that my liver was fine, my kidneys were fine, and that some count, taken during my first check had been 67, the danger level was 60, but it was now down to a normal 30, I replied, "I have so much to be thankful for." He then answered, "I went to a lecture in London recently, and a professor stated that if patients said, 'Thank you', and showed a positive attitude, their chances of recovery were much greater. Saying, 'thank you', makes a patient less likely to be depressed, worried and anxious, and has the effect of killing off some of the nasties in their body." We were talking of cancer, but a positive attitude is the only way through, no matter what is happening to you, and I would add to that, a positive attitude in Jesus can work miracles.

In Jesus, "I am more than conqueror." I have faced cancer, twice, coped with all the Charlies and drunken sailors that came my way, faced financial hardship, bought long curtains at a ridiculous price, not been "scarred" because a doctor was "off colour" on one of my check ups, found the strength to say, "No," when necessary, and, "Yes," when necessary. I enjoy life to the full, and rejoice in the love of my husband, family, and friends, and have held a baby in my arms I never expected to see. The list is as endless as the love of Jesus. No matter what, in Jesus "We are more than conquerors." Even if, as a result of a tumour of the lung, I had died, the answer would be the same, because in Jesus, "I am more than conqueror." But only in Him, because through the Cross of Calvary He has had conquered sin and death and this truth has set me free. Death has no hold over me, for, "If the truth will make you free, you will be free indeed." Praise God ... what a Saviour!

Read the Gospels for yourself; sort it out now, while you still have time. If reading my book has enabled you to know the truth of the above paragraph, then I just thank God, because I believe He wanted me to write it. But on no account should you worry, the order of the day is trust, not worry. You are so precious in God's sight, "He has written your name on the palm of His hand." You are absolutely safe. The devil would have you anxious and afraid, but not Jesus, He loves you, just as you are, and says, "My peace I give you, my peace I leave with you, do not let your hearts be troubled and do not be afraid." That is the word of a gentleman, the Son of God.

As one of my favourite texts puts it: -

"Have no anxiety about anything, but in everything by prayer and supplication, with thanksgiving, let your requests be made known to God.

And the peace of God, which passes all understanding, will keep your hearts and minds in Christ Jesus!"
(Philippians 4: 6,7)

The Family Group

The Hailsham Parish Church Magazine for March 1998 contained the following paragraphs under the heading 'In Memoriam':

'Grace Hulbert
'What a service of celebration and thanksgiving we held to remember Grace last month!

'Hugh and the family had brought together many strands of her life and wove them into a joyous and uplifting service.

'Glyn Griffiths sang solo "Jesus Stand Among Us" to set the scene. Following a favourite hymn, "Be Still For the Presence of the Lord", the Vicar spoke of Grace and her crown. Two of her children, Paul and Ruth, sang a favourite chorus ("Be With Me Lord Every Hour of the Day."

'Adrian Plass then had us with the usual 'aching sides' as he spoke of Grace as a friend. More singing followed with Fran and friends. Grace's son Martin then spoke of Grace and focused on her faith. An augmented choir sang Stainer's "God so Loved the World."

'That was followed by prayers (led by Wendy Pugh) and a reading (from Romans 8) by son-in-law Mark. Hugh rounded off the service and we concluded with "Thine be the Glory, Risen Conquering Son." We had thanked God for His grace and Hugh's Grace. She will always be our Grace.'

A further entry in the same magazine read: 'Hugh Hulbert and his family want to express their heartfelt gratitude for the loving support, the many lovely cards and letters, and the assurances of prayer that they have received since the homecall of their beloved Grace. Thank you too for coming to the memorial service and helping to make it such a wonderful occasion, glorifying the name of our Lord Jesus Christ. The contributions in word, anthem and song, on the organ and on other instruments, and the simple fact of your presence, were all most sincerely appreciated - not forgetting the bountiful provision made for us all in the lounge afterwards. It is such a joy to be associated with the family of God at St Mary's and Emmanuel.'

In our 1997 Christmas letter we had written: 'The second half of the year has been particularly difficult for Grace and our movements have been restricted from the time of her birthday in July. Infections which have not responded to antibiotics and some surgery in November have left her very weak and often breathless. A further "bleep" in the past few weeks prevents us making any definite Christmas plans ..."

A further stay in the Eastbourne hospital became necessary in January and then the end came quite quickly. On Tuesday, February 3rd, at 1.30 am, with Hugh and Martin at her bedside, Just Grace passed peacefully into the immediate presence of her glorious Saviour to be 'forever with the Lord'.